CW01496527

MY MAYENNE

James Barrie

MINERVA PRESS
LONDON
MIAMI   RIO DE JANEIRO   DELHI

MY MAYENNE
Copyright © James Barrie 2000

All Rights Reserved

No part of this book may be reproduced in any form
by photocopying or by any electronic or mechanical means,
including information storage or retrieval systems,
without permission in writing from both the copyright
owner and the publisher of this book.

ISBN 0 75411 007 9

First Published 2000 by
MINERVA PRESS
315–317 Regent Street
London W1R 7YB

Printed in Great Britain for Minerva Press

September 2001

With best wishes

James Barrie

MY MAYENNE

Acknowledgements

These could be almost as long as the book! First of all, thanks go to all those who both knowingly and unknowingly have been a part of the book. Thanks to all those from P&O who looked after all our toings and froings, in particular Jo, who coped with our bookings and always kept her cool, and Tracy, who was always cheerful. I must also thank and acknowledge my younger daughter who always managed to find the things that I had lost on my computer and prevented me from deleting the whole book, and finally my wife, who not only had to listen to my ramblings but had to read them as well!

Chapter I

Why My Mayenne? Well, I found it. Nobody else (not even in France, apart from the locals) seems to know where it is and they don't want it anyway! So, by basic logic, it's mine. QED – quite easily done – as my old Maths master used to say.

I have holidayed in France, with my wife and children, constantly for twenty-five years and for a time had a house in Calvados. We loved the drink (Calva to the locals), and also the cider and the cheese, in particular the Pont l'Evêque, but somehow we were never particularly happy or at ease there. Mayenne is very different – the biggest problem we have is trying to contain the constant flow of invitations to have lunchtime drinks and even afternoon teas. What it is going to be like when we are living there permanently heaven knows. There'll be drinks here and drinks there, both of which you dare not refuse because you may offend.

In the seventies we decided that we would like to settle around Bordeaux – my main reason being that I would be close to the Médoc and St Émilion and endless other good wines, many of which are still thankfully unknown. My wife, on the other hand, had much better reasons – the pleasant environment, nice people, warm climate and then, good beaches. I am not saying that I don't appreciate those things as well, but I think, if I am honest, that good wine is more important to me!

We looked, as many holidaymakers do, in the windows of countless *agences immobilières*, but never ventured to go in! At this stage we just wanted to know what was available on the market and get some idea of the prices. We thought that we would try and find something that needed renovation, not realising that most of these types of properties are sold by the local *notaire*. We felt that by buying something that needed renovation we would get a better deal and feel we had achieved something by returning a dwelling – a chateau, perhaps – to its original splendour! Were these pipe dreams? They weren't really as we really *did* want to do it. What stopped us at this stage was the realisation that we had to be practical – the time was not yet right. We had three children at that time, all at school, and the maximum amount of time that we could hope to spend in France was five weeks a year.

However practical and realistic we were trying to be, our dreams would not go away. The years went by and we yearned for a place of our own in France. We had never seriously considered the Dordogne or Provence, delightful though they both are, largely because of the travel involved in getting there. We were also beginning to abandon our thoughts of the Bordeaux area. Oh my beloved Médoc and St Émilion – how I would miss them! There were two main reasons for rejecting those areas – the first was that there were too many English people living there, but the second, and probably far more important reason, was that they were too far from the ports of Le Havre and Cherbourg. At this stage of our lives this latter point was very important. I could not afford to retire to France, at least not yet, but we wanted to spend as much time in France as possible. The conclusion had to be that any house or ruin that we bought really had to be within a two-hour drive of either Le Havre or Cherbourg if we were going to be able to make full use of it. We had now begun to take our holidays in Eastern Brittany and Normandy, with only the occasional visit to my beloved Bordeaux. Things began to fall into place and the inevitable happened – we started yet again to look into the windows of the *agences immobilières*. But now we had progressed – we began to venture inside! We looked around Dinan, Dinard and St-Malo and had conducted tours with various agents who were convinced that every property we saw we were going to buy. Saying that you like a property is akin to saying that you wish to buy – the agent then tries to whisk you off to his pet *notaire* so you can sign a binding agreement!

We decided that picturesque though these places were, the houses were probably out of our price range, even though at the time the exchange rate was ten francs to the pound. We were going to have to look further inland. This decision caused us to focus on Combourg, a small market town south east of Le Mont St Michel where there were several good *agences immobilières* in addition to a splendid medieval castle and two good restaurants.

On one particular visit to Combourg, the friendly *agent immobilier* took us to see six properties, all of which were in need of renovation, restoration and, in some cases, a total rebuild – some were just rather large piles of very useable stone! The prices varied from fifty thousand to two hundred thousand francs. It appeared that, just as in England, the more that you were prepared to pay the better the value you got for your money. For instance, for fifty thousand francs you would get a habitable building, well for camping out in anyway, comprising two up and two down, without much land and with no main services, not even a privy in sight. But there would be water and electricity close at hand. For two hundred thousand francs, on the other hand, you would get a four-bedroom house, with say an acre of land, and with electricity and water connected but no mains drainage. It would be habitable but would need a lot of modernisation and general tidying up. These prices relate to the mid-eighties, although if you look around, talk to the locals, are prepared to bargain and do not employ the services of the *agent immobilier* (remember, it is the purchaser who pays the commission, not the seller, in France), then you can still find property at these sorts of prices.

It was an enjoyable day, an experience that both my wife and myself will not forget in a hurry, particularly given what followed. The agent had given us a lot of his time, and, in his words, had shown us six 'interesting' properties. Which one of the six did we wish to buy? I said that my wife and I would need time to think before we could make any firm commitment. It very quickly became apparent that he did not warm to this. I looked at my watch and said that we had to leave as we had a boat to catch. This was not entirely true, as we were not leaving France for a couple of days, but at least it gave us a chance to make a rapid exit. I had made the mistake of giving him one of my business cards so we were not to make the clean break that I had been hoping for. However, it did mean that we would not dare call on the services of that *agent immobilier* again.

In another agent's window my wife had seen a property that she liked the look of – a small but derelict slaughterhouse (which we hoped had not been used for many years!) in the middle of nowhere. But this time there were actually directions in the window explaining how to get there and even an indication of the price – this was most unusual in our experience to date. Clearly this *agent immobilier* was not going to waste his time taking prospective purchasers out to see it. He was just going to leave them to their own devices and wait for the offers, if any, to come rolling in. As it was close to the route back to our caravan I agreed that there was no harm in going to have a look. What a sucker I am! Yes, she fell for it – it was just what she had always wanted! Within minutes she had outlined plans for its conversion into a four-bedroom house, whilst I walked around the building observing the rather large cracks in the walls, some of which, even to a non-surveyor, looked quite recent. I was wondering if, once one started converting and, in particular, making any structural alterations, there would be any of the original building still standing. Would one end up with just a building plot! But she would not be put off and was already planning the garden of her new-found gem! It was one hundred and fifty thousand francs and, I felt, a complete rip-off in comparison with everything else that we had seen to date, but I knew that at this stage to question her judgement (who said sanity?) would be more than my life was worth. I just said, 'It looks very interesting but I think we ought to go now as I am feeling both hungry and thirsty.' Fortunately, she agreed.

A few days later we returned to England but on the journey my wife still had the slaughterhouse very much on her mind and had reached the drawing-board stage. I said nothing. I don't know what happened after that. I am sure it was nothing I did or said, but all of a sudden she said that she wasn't interested in it anymore and even took things a stage further by saying that perhaps England wasn't so bad after – and we could leave France alone, apart from holidays.

As you can probably guess, the cooling-off period did not last, or at least not for long! Once you get the bug it won't go away. Almost as inevitably as night follows day, our first venture into French property followed. It was more by chance than design.

In the mid-eighties we acquired the lease of an already tastefully converted property, largely because it had a very well-fitted kitchen. This was in the Calvados region of Normandy. It was a large house on three floors, with two bathrooms and seven bedrooms, all tastefully decorated. This was unusual for France, certainly in our experience. The most important thing in a French house appears to be the television – the bigger it is, the more affluent you are. We liked the house in many ways but yet we didn't – it's hard to explain. It may have been because under the terms of the lease we could not alter it to any significant degree and thus put our individual stamp on it. However, it served its purpose. We now had a base in France and spent some very enjoyable holidays and short breaks there. It convinced us that we wanted to live in France. One thing that did puzzle us was that we had difficulty building any relationships with the villagers. They treated 'Les Anglais' with suspicion. It may have been because of the previous owners – who knows.

After nearly four years we decided to get rid of it and to go in active search of the 'real thing'. This is where the story really begins. This time it would be something old – the older the better – a house that we could really get our teeth into and eventually restore to its original state.

We never thought that we would find anything really old that would also fulfil all our requirements and yet still be within our price range, but we eventually did. It was in the Mayenne, or the upper Loire region, if you want to sound posh! It was clearly waiting for us – it was steeped in history, had been virtually untouched for centuries and was possibly up to nine hundred years old! The house, we believe, had been a retreat for the abbot and other monks from Le Mont St Michel.

Now the story can begin. I hope it will give you as many laughs as it has given us – ours in hindsight, yours as you read the book. Also the problems that you encounter when you take on a challenge like this – buying and then restoring a house which is about nine hundred years old and which has not been inhabited for about three hundred years – apart from bats, owls and various rodents and the farmer smoking his pigs up the chimney. Just remember, nothing is insurmountable. A project such as this has to be approached with patience. The degree of satisfaction that it gives you as you proceed, just cannot be measured!

Chapter II

Things took a serious turn in 1992. My three older children had all left home and my wife decided that it had to be now or never if we were to find our dream wreck in France. You must be beginning to think that it is my wife who makes all the decisions! Well, it's not – I just let her think that she does. This gives me the added advantage that if things go wrong, which fortunately they do not, I can always blame her. Her suggestion was really very logical. She wanted to start on something now, while I was still fit enough to shin up and down ladders, hump plasterboard about, mix cement and concrete and be able to see well enough to do the wiring and plumbing. This was very sensible, but I still have an underlying feeling that my wife would still have me doing those things fit or not! What I have omitted to say is that she works just as hard as I do – plastering, cementing and building drystone walls. That's a thought – I think I will hire her out when I am no longer fit for work!

Where should we start? We had already decided to be practical and find a house within two hours of Le Havre – there are better boats from Portsmouth to Le Havre than to Cherbourg. Another reason was the fare structure and the very regular service, in addition to the fact that a journey to England, for whatever reason, would be very easy.

I suppose in addition to this there is my belt-and-braces approach to life – never abandon anything totally because you never know just when you might need it and always leave yourself with an alternative in case you change your mind.

Hence we decided to begin by looking in Normandy, and possibly in Brittany and other adjacent areas. At this stage we had never heard of the Mayenne, apart from the town of that name, and although we had driven through it at one time or another, we knew nothing about it. What should we do? For a start, where should we look? We had gone off the idea of doing a tour of the *agences immobilières*, primarily because we did not quite know in which area we should be looking. The other problem we found was that by and large they only showed you what they wanted to show you rather than doing a search on your behalf linked to your requirements.

There are a number of agents in London who advertise nationally regarding property in France, but we felt that with the sort of property we were looking for they would be unlikely to be able to help us because in sheer economic terms there would not be enough commission in it for them. We thought of running an advert ourselves but doubted whether that would be successful. Where do people with cheaper properties for sale in France advertise? The answer, believe it or not, is in *Exchange and Mart*. The adverts by and large tend to be English estate agents who act for English agents/wheeler-dealers in France. During one particular week in May 1993, there were six such ads and I phoned/faxed all of them. Interestingly, of the six, only two fulfilled the criteria that I had given them. The rest of them sent us details of every single property that they had in France from Nice to Calais at prices of up to five million francs. As a result of this we were put in touch with an English agent in Normandy and began dealing with him directly. This was Pierre Médoc, so called because he was always better after he had finished the second bottle. Within two weeks, we had made contact and were on our way to Normandy to visit the trusty Pierre. After the customary two bottles of Médoc (I did not know that it was customary at this stage) – which I supplied, he began to warm to us and decided that he was sure that he could help. In fact, he felt sure that he had the ideal property for us. We went though an album full of photographs and a pile of details and every time I said 'I really like that one,' he would say, 'What a shame, I have just sold that one – what a pity that you didn't come last week'. I was beginning to despair when he said that there were lots of others to show us but they had only just come on the market and he hadn't had time to photograph them yet.

We returned to our hotel that night – please note, no touring caravan, a bit of civilisation and comfort – having had a very convivial afternoon and evening but with some doubts as to whether or not this was the best way to approach the property market.

Nonetheless we had arranged for him to pick us up at nine o'clock the next morning and all we could do was to hope for the best, like Mr Micawbar. Something would turn up.

For much of the day we visited an assortment of oversized hen houses, vast chateaux with no roofs and few supporting walls and derelict farmhouses. Each one seemed better than the previous one (was this a part of the ploy?), but there was nothing, at least not as yet, that I felt comfortable with, although there were several that my wife, with her vivid imagination (being an artist), decided were perfect and which her 'I can do anything husband' could turn into something fantastic. It was nice that she felt that way, but I was doggedly unmoved.

I was convinced that something somewhere out there would be right for us, but could Pierre really help us or would we have to start all over again? My apparent disappointment did not seem to worry him and he suggested that we go further afield. Pierre dealt mainly with Normandy properties, primarily because he did not have to travel too far to visit them and secondly because he was also a builder and it is easier to organise and get things done within your own patch.

However, he wanted a sale and it quickly became clear that his approach was, 'You want something – I will find you just what you want!' Because of this we moved just out of Normandy to – you've guessed it – the Mayenne, also known as the Pays de Loire. The first house that he showed us was much more interesting – a terrace with four buildings, once lived in, which could be converted very easily into one nice house and two small cottages. It had a nice walled garden and was situated in a small hamlet of six or seven other houses. The price was one hundred and thirty thousand francs about fifteen thousand pounds at the time. I quite liked it and could visualise it finished. My wife on the other hand felt that it was a bit claustrophobic. We decided that we might make an offer, but when we did we found out that the property was owned by four brothers and two sisters – the brothers wanted to sell but the sisters did not! Because of these doubts we did not sit around and withdrew our offer. Interestingly, three years on it is still for sale we are told.

So far, so bad! We wanted but we could not find. What should we do next? Our short trip was all but over and we had little to show for it. This made Pierre all the more determined. He had already summed me up as being 'a likeable eccentric' and was thus even more determined to find the right property for us. I took this as a compliment as I have a book signed by the author Peter Ustinov in which he wrote 'To Jim, the self-confessed eccentric, from Peter'. Although I have never fully read the book I treasure the inscription!

We returned to England, not depressed or downhearted but just wondering where we would go from here. One evening, within a week of our return, a well-Médoc'd Pierre telephoned to say that he had just the property for us. It was perfect in every way, and apparently only my wife and I would be interested in it – only my wife and I would buy it. He added as a sting in the tail, 'My partner says that this property is unsellable – now there's a challenge.'

That sort of comment would put any normal mortal off, but not us. Yes, you have guessed it – in a little over a week we were back in France. We were full of hope but apprehensive, hoping that Pierre would not let us down.

When we arrived, all full of enthusiasm, we found that Pierre was not available. I cannot remember why or just where he had gone, but his eldest son had been left with all the details of how to get there. However, he had no pictures, rundown on the property or any idea of the price. We hoped that the end of the day would be better than the beginning.

Again the property was in the Mayenne, about eighteen kilometres from Bagnoles-de-l'Orne and quite close to the terraced barns that we had already seen. He decided that we should go by the scenic route, or perhaps that was the only way he knew of reaching the property. I'm sure that's not true – it's just me being cynical! On the way he discovered a picture of the property, he thought, together with some brief details and a price. It looked interesting but it was difficult to estimate just how large (or small) it was.

We duly arrived outside a large double-barn complex about one hundred feet long and forty feet wide.

'This is it,' said the son and heir.

It didn't look like it at all to me as the photograph indicated that it was on sloping ground. When I voiced my doubts he said that perhaps his father had put the wrong details in with the photo, or vice versa.

'Are there any other properties around here that it could be?' I asked.

'Unlikely,' he said, but my persistence and doubts paid off as I looked further down the road. I travelled barely two hundred yards, sorry, I mean metres, down the road when lo and behold I came across a complex of other farm buildings. Here was the large building on the sloping ground. It looked both austere and unkempt, but yet it had presence. I don't know that I'm terribly good at determining the age of buildings from the outside, except if there are turrets and/or archways, and by the shape and design of the windows, but this building was giving away few secrets, apart from an arched stone doorway. But yet somehow, I don't know why, I just felt that this building was very old.

The door within the stone arch was a patched, ill-fitting, stable door – patched with part of a galvanised iron sheet. The main window, or what remained of it, had suffered a similar fate and was also patched with fertiliser bags where there was no glass. We pushed the door open, revealing a very large room with a high-beamed ceiling and an absolutely enormous fireplace. It was all very dark and dirty. Eventually I found a single light switch, which when I pressed down gave me a shock as a reward. But a single, solitary light did come on. Immediately the size and the proportions of the room became apparent – it was vast! The room was about twenty-five feet long, with a ten- to twelve-foot beamed ceiling. I had never seen such beams – they must have been twenty-one inches high and fifteen inches wide. Two of them ran the full length of the room with so many six by six-inch beams in between that there were just too many to count. The fireplace was a typical Breton one, some twelve feet wide. It was supported on carved, receding pillars with a chimney opening nearly three feet in depth. The chimney some thirty feet high from within, went straight up with daylight above – relatively easy to clean if you have a wide enough brush. On the opposite side of the room was a high wooden wall which ran from floor to ceiling – how on earth did you get upstairs? There was no time to think about that now as there were still things to explore downstairs. At the far end of the room was a low arched doorway, complete with wooden door, which led into a room of much smaller proportions – seven-foot beamed ceiling and a room size of fifteen by ten feet. This, although quite old, was clearly a later addition. It was here that I found the electricity supply with one thin wire coming out to our solitary light. There was also a thick black cable disappearing through the outside wall. I wondered where that went – that was a surprise in store and yet to be revealed!

Returning to the main room – what could one call it – it was not a lounge or a dining room, but perhaps a reception hall, we moved to the right under a low stone arch down what was almost a small tunnel (only eight feet long) into a cellar of the same proportions as the main room but with a much lower ceiling. I am just under six feet tall and even I had to duck under the two main beams. What a lovely wine cellar it would make, I thought, but I did not utter a word. My wife on the other hand, voiced her opinion.

'What a lovely kitchen/dining room/snug it would make, and even a small corner for your wine!'

It's funny how our priorities differ! What intrigued me was that the room was a perfect square – that led me to wonder about the main room. Just what was behind that high wooden wall. Now was the time to find out!

Working back along this high wall, which I now realised was probably made from heavy tongued and grooved timbers, I eventually discovered a well-concealed door, also made from tongued and grooved timbers, with a tiny, almost invisible latch. The door was well and truly stuck, but when I managed to prise it open there was a wonderful carved staircase some twenty feet in length – it just had to be oak. It went up to the next floor. What a find! We gingerly climbed the stairs, not knowing quite how safe they were. But we needn't have worried – rickety the staircase may have been but the timbers were most definitely sound.

At the top of the stairs, we had a choice. We could go two steps down to the left to one room, three steps up in front to another, or four steps up to the right to another. Decisions, decisions – two steps were easier so we went to the left. There was another enormous room, of similar proportions to the main room downstairs. Again it had a very high-beamed ceiling, probably higher than the one downstairs. There were just ten beams going the length of the room, each twenty-five feet long and a foot by a foot. No wonder there is a shortage of trees in the area! This is not really fair, but it must have taken quite a number to construct the building. Here was another magnificent fireplace – it was not quite of the proportions of the one downstairs, but of a similar design. To the right, within the fireplace, was a headless statue. Who could it be – the Madonna or Joan of Arc? The latter had a lot of influence in the area. The house got more impressive all the time, although there were far fewer rooms than we had envisaged from looking at the outside. Moving out of this room and to the left and up the three stairs we entered an attic area above the extension below. My wife had already envisaged the latter as a possible kitchen, if she could not have the cellar. This attic area would make one or possibly two bathrooms. Quickly moving out of here and up four more stairs we entered a very large open area, the size of the room downstairs, which went right up to the eaves. There is not much to say about it really, apart from the fact that there was yet another magnificent fireplace. If we ever bought this house it would have to be very carefully and lovingly restored, and any subdividing of rooms would have to be done very sympathetically. Leaving this room, still moving upwards, we climbed a short, rather rugged, staircase, with no sign of a banister, and entered a vast attic. Judging from the missing pane of glass in the skylight and the large droppings under one of the beams, it must have been the home of the resident owl! At least it had probably kept the number of mice running around down to a minimum.

So that was it. What were our thoughts? To say they were muddled I think would be an understatement. It was nothing at all like we had anticipated, or I suppose quite what we were looking for, but yet we found it appealing. Standing outside and looking at it again we felt that we liked it and the general feeling of peace and tranquillity that it had, but were we capable of tackling something like this? It was totally different from anything we had ever worked on before. Clearly no decisions could be made that day, but would a time delay and talking about it really help us to come to a decision?

We were still very muddled when we drove away from the building, wanting to turn around when we were less than a kilometre away to take another look but knowing that that was not going to solve the problem. As a distraction, we were shown some other properties on the way back that we had not seen before, but as you can guess our thoughts were miles away.

Back to England and reality! We were really in a dreadful muddle and finding it totally impossible to come to any decisions, even though we knew that probably the rational and most sensible decision to make was to forget it because of the sheer immensity of the task.

Alas we are not the sort of people who make rational and sensible decisions – it takes the fun out of life if you are! We look around at so many of our friends and think what dull and uninteresting lives they lead. They may have security, or as much as they can reasonably expect in this world, but what dull lives they lead – the same old routine day in and day out. In all probability they plan next year's holiday as soon as they get back from this year's, just waiting until they retire, as if that is going to be the solution to all their problems instead of the start of a whole series of new ones. They won't have a clue as to what to do with their new-found leisure time. Not for us!

Sorry, I'm rambling again! To hell with it, I thought, we'd go ahead with it. I telephoned the Médoc man who was very pleased to hear from me. He also gave me some surprising but very welcome news. Had we realised that in addition to the house, included in the price, were two adjacent barns plus a quarter of an acre of garden? And had we seen the magnificent bread oven in the attached building? Being totally mesmerised, we had not taken any of this in! And as an added bonus the price had been reduced by ten thousand francs.

In France, once you have committed yourself things move fast. Or rather, the *notaire* would have liked it all signed and sealed before we could say the word Mayenne! Pierre was already talking about an immediate ten per cent deposit and completion within the month!

Quick decision makers we may be, but in a situation like this we would not be bulldozed. We took our time, but actually decided against using an English solicitor. My main reason for deciding this was that our house had probably not been inhabited for three hundred years and so there would be no debts/liabilities for us to take over – something about which you have to be careful when buying French property. You take over the liabilities as well as the assets! The choice has to be yours with regards to taking legal advice. In our case nothing went wrong, but it would have been a very different matter if it had done.

Chapter III

The purchase of the property went through, albeit very slowly, as there were queries from both sides. It possibly went more slowly than it would have done had I employed a solicitor, but really in the sort of deal that we were doing there were no potential pitfalls. At least when one was doing it oneself one was totally in the picture all the time and inevitably saving money. I don't know why, but once you mention 'property abroad' to a solicitor the costs on a pro rata basis seem almost to double. This is not me being cynical – I did make some preliminary enquiries. The purchase should be quite straightforward as long as you make sure that:

(a) the seller has good title to the property and

(b) there are no debts attached to the property either by the owner or any of his tenants. Under French law, if there are, then you become liable.

Fortunately for us, in this case there weren't any.

My wife anticipated that it would take some time before we completed the deal and also had the foresight to see that it would be a minimum of twelve months after that before we could move into what was now going to be known as Le Manoir. Accordingly, she went around caravan hunting. In a very short space of time she had discovered an Elddis for us. It was small but very well equipped, with mains electricity, a full-size fridge and a new stove with some minor body damage – all for the princely sum of four hundred and fifty pounds. This was bought before I could blow my nose, let alone question the transaction, and much to my amazement pound notes were being passed. I shall have to check my wallet more frequently.

As soon as the deposit was paid on the house in the October, our bargain was hitched up and we were on our way to France. We didn't have a clue where we were going to place it until the sale was finalised, but at this stage we didn't care as we imagined it would be only a few weeks! Just as in England, most of the campsites close down at the end of September and the first three turned us away. At the fourth, however, I managed in my limited French, which was rapidly improving, to convince a charming French lady to let us stay on her site for just a few days. There was relief all round, although her husband, when he returned in the evening was none too pleased and told me that we would have to go.

'Fine,' I said, 'as long as you direct me to a campsite that is open.'

He could not and, as a result, reluctantly agreed that we could stay for a maximum of three nights. I wonder if it was the bottle of whisky which my wife produced from the caravan that helped him change his mind? We shall never know!

Somehow we did not seem to have written this possible difficulty into our plans – who says we are impulsive? It was clearly not going to be easy to find a campsite. Then the rescue came. Pierre Médoc – he was bound to turn up trumps and he did –is well worth two bottles of Médoc every time I see him. That night I phoned Pierre who said, 'No problem – you can leave it at Carrier Bags's house.' To question Pierre at that time when he was being so helpful would have been a mistake, so we arranged to call around the following day to see him and his wife and whichever of his six children happened to be around. We were both very puzzled as to who or what Carrier Bags might be, but who were we to ask questions? We were just both very grateful! Arriving at Pierre's, very soon after he had consumed his second glass of good wine, (incidentally there is no such thing as bad wine in France – some of it is just better/a bit worse than others!) he told us all about Carrier Bags. He was a client of Pierre's who had been trying to purchase a property in France for years and the one that he had finally settled for was where our caravan was to rest. You have probably guessed correctly – he was very much a cash customer. He always carried two carrier bags – one filled with his worldly possessions and the other with money! Pierre used to say that Carrier Bags thought that this way, with a bag full of cash, he would get a better deal, not having worked out that Pierre would not only have checked how much was in the carrier bag and charged him accordingly, but would also have ensured that there was enough left over for him to be taken out to a nice meal, with lots of brandy afterwards!

Anyway, it was unlikely that Carrier Bags would be over for at least six months, possibly more. If he came any earlier he would get a nasty shock as Pierre had not started on his conversion yet! Thus we were very welcome to stay there whilst we waited for our purchase to be completed. I could plug into his electricity supply and there was water from the well. An additional advantage was that it was only twenty kilometres from our home-to-be.

Pierre's wife gave us directions to the house. It all sounded very simple and clear me, so just how we almost ended up in a duck pond unable to reverse the caravan, I'm not quite sure. To say that I got angry would perhaps be polite – I exploded as the smell of burning clutch got worse and the caravan gradually dug a hole for itself in the soft ground. What made it worse was the fact that I am supposed to be quite a skilful map reader and good at following directions! I realised that swearing and cursing were not going to get me anywhere and after half an hour (it seemed like three hours!) of pulling and pushing and getting distinctly out of breath, my wife and I, with the encouragement of our ten-year-old daughter (oh to have had the hefty sons around!) who is exceptionally good at pouring oil on troubled waters, eventually managed to turn the caravan around sufficiently to be able to tow it out. Having got out of this, I immediately wanted to phone Pierre.

'That's not going to solve anything,' said my wife, calmly. 'He's tucked up in bed, and if he were awake would only laugh at you. Let's sit in the car, re-read the directions and see if we have mis-read them or if there is any part of them which could have been interpreted differently.' This we did and we came across something near the end which was ambiguous. Interpreting what Pierre's wife had said in an alternative way, we reckoned that we had found where we should have been, if you see what I mean. We went just twenty metres further down the road and turned left and felt con-fident that we were now on the right road (track!). Our confidence was rewarded. Within a matter of minutes, with great relief, we were there. The situation was just how it had been described although the cottage was much smaller than we had envisaged – we reckoned that the whole house would have gone inside the reception hall/lounge of Le Manoir!

During this visit, and many more over the next nine months, we never saw Carrier Bags and even began to wonder if he did exist or was just an idea in the mind of God i.e. Pierre. We visited Le Manoir on many occasions, both taking measurements and generally making an appraisal of what needed to be done. Trying to prioritise this was a virtually impossible task. When the weather was dull we hated it and used to mumble, 'What on earth are we doing in this dark, eerie building?' But when the sun was shining everything was different. No wonder depression rates almost double in wintertime!

So the summer proceeded. We made many short visits to France but our frustrations continued – we still had not taken possession of Le Manoir. We had loads of ideas, had written pages and pages of things that needed to be done and my wife had made innumerable drawings of how things could/should look.

At last we had the telephone call for which we had been waiting: the *notaire* was in receipt of all the documentation and the moneys. The latter was of course much more important than the former. The property was ours! We wondered if the seller knew.

We arranged to travel from Portsmouth to Le Havre – thank you, P&O (pleasant and often in our vocabulary) – propelled by our faithful Tipo and towing the box trailer. The journey, fortunately, was uneventful. We went straight to Le Manoir and, hardly pausing to unhitch the trailer, were off to collect the caravan. As anticipated, there was no sign of Carrier Bags nor any evidence of work on the conversion! At 1 a.m. we were back and the caravan was duly parked. It was not quite as easy as that, but it was certainly easier than towing it out of the duck pond situation. We had no time or inclination to do any unpacking. We literally crawled into the caravan and slumped into bed, far too tired to look at the house or to do anything else.

Although I am normally an early riser, on the following morning I was not up until eight o'clock. On second thoughts, it *was* quite early as that was French time. My brain, muddled though it was at that stage, was telling me that it was only seven o'clock. Ah well, I ought to be able to adjust – as for the first time in all my working life I was going to have a whole month's holiday. What a joke! Some rapid transformations had to take place in that time, so there would hardly be any time for a rest, unless, that is, I could think of a good excuse! That should not have been too difficult, but the problem was this: would the queen – the ultimate ruler and decision maker – accept my reasons?

Leaving the caravan as quietly as I could, so that I did not disturb my wife and daughter's slumbers, I tripped over the caravan step and more or less fell into the car. I had chance to hear the weather forecast (why are we British so obsessed with weather – according to my old mum it's not because our weather is so rotten but because we are born optimists and we are always hoping that the sun will shine tomorrow) and the news.

Quietly sitting, clad in my non-flattering pyjamas (definitely not designer wear!), I was startled by a tapping on the roof of the car. Standing outside, peering at me, was a greying Frenchman with a serious look on his face. What on earth did he want at this time of day and just who was he? After all, it was not his land – it was ours! At least that is what I had been led to understand. I explained to this stranger just who I was and he told me that he already knew! Then I told him that I had bought the property.

He replied, 'No, you are *buying* the property.'

It was amazing that I understood all this in French.

'No, no,' I said, trying not to look or to sound anxious. 'We have paid the *notaire* – the transaction was completed five days ago.'

With that he disappeared rapidly, together with his wife. Less than half an hour later, even though it was a Sunday, I saw his car parked outside the local *notaire*'s as I went to buy my croissants and baguettes.

My wife and daughter were both totally unaware of all that had been going on. They were just sleeping the sleep of the just!

An hour later the grey-headed Frenchman, who was of course the farmer who had sold me the buildings, returned, but this time he was smiling. He shook me by the hand, introduced me to his wife and said that the *notaire* had told him that everything had been completed and that I could take possession. It was fait accompli! He then asked us around to his house for aperitifs at noon. At this stage this was the last thing that I wanted, but I realised I could not even consider refusing because of the mortal wound that I would be inflicting. I thanked him warmly for his kindness and they left me in peace.

By this time my wife and daughter had emerged, totally unaware of the crisis/problems that I had endured whilst they were still pursuing their slumbers.

'What I am looking forward to,' said my wife, 'is spending the day relaxing, unwinding and working out just where we are going to start.'

The unpacking was taken totally for granted! Dare I tell her? By this time you may be beginning to imagine that my wife is a dragon. She is most definitely not – she just breathes fire from time to time. I took a big deep breath. 'How do you fancy a quiet drink at lunchtime?' I asked, trying to make it sound as casual as possible.

'That would be nice,' came the reply.

Another and much deeper breath and I said, 'With the farmer and his wife?'

'You haven't, have you?' she asked, making the assumption that in my usual sociable way I had asked them around to Le Manoir – as if I would have. Be that as it may, she took an awful lot of convincing and then realised that she was in a catch-22 situation!

'A chance to improve your French, dear,' I said and quickly ducked as half a baguette went flying past my ear. It was not the first part of the sentence that had upset her – it was being referred to as 'dear'. She keeps reminding me, but alas to no avail as I keep forgetting that she is not a 'dear'. She is a darling!

My daughter thought that this was all rather funny until I reminded her that she was the one who was learning French and who would not only have to speak in French but translate as well. She turned ashen until she realised that (possibly) I was joking, but went to find her Larousse to be on the safe side. She couldn't find it anywhere. What she did not know was that her father had already decided it was a must for our meeting with the farmer and had put it in his pocket so that he would not forget it! Honestly, I am not always that mean – ask the family. On second thoughts don't!

We unpacked the trailer and the car and wandered around the house and overgrown grounds unable to concentrate because of our impending social engagement. My wife and daughter suddenly said, with one voice, 'What should I wear?'

Is it that important? I thought. I said, 'We are not exactly having an audience with the Queen!' They did not want to hear this and eventually decisions were made.

We arrived at the farmer's house. It was not his main house as he lives mainly in Paris (we think he is a professional cornet player!) and comes down to tend his crops – a totally arable farm – from time to time. He was pacing up and down outside, possibly because he thought that we might not come (because we had not understood what he had said), or because he wanted to make sure that we parked in the right place or to make us welcome – or all three.

After the shaking of hands we were ushered into the kitchen/diner, which was typically French (apart from the fact that there was no television – very untypical!) It was very bare and what I suppose my wife would call 'somewhat basic'. Madame was there with bottles of grenadine, *pastis* and water on the table together with little biscuits. Being a whisky drinker I asked for *pastis* on its own and then quickly wished that I had not. It is real firewater – you live and learn! It lacked the smoothness of a good whisky and rather burnt the back of my throat. My wife had grenadine, with a dash of water, whilst my daughter sensibly went for orange juice – they were doing better than me. We stayed for an hour, which on the first visit was probably about the right length of time.

To the surprise of both parties, we managed to hold quite a meaningful conversation during our visit. The first topic of conversation was the thunderstorm the night before, not that we had really been aware of it after our journey. Somehow I could not remember all the words, that is assuming that I had ever known them. My wife solved the problem by saying 'boom, bang a bang', whilst I fumbled for my phrase book. After that things got easier and, with the aid of a second *pastis*, this time with water, I found that not only was I making myself understood but I could also understand most of what our farmer friend was saying. My French has improved a lot since that day, but I still feel that I have a long way to go.

We talked about the birds and other wild animals, learning a lot of new vocabulary all the time, and then came the amusing incident. Without knowing its name I was trying to describe a hedge-hog. After some minutes our host eventually said, '*Ah, un hérisson*.' Then I attempted to explain both verbally and with actions – the mind boggles – that in England it is called a 'hedgehog'. My eventual definition was 'a pig in a wood'. He, naturally, fell about laughing. I felt that after this, our friendship was cemented. We left feeling a little bit inadequate, not knowing at the time that our French friends, who spoke no English at all, had thoroughly enjoyed the experience and had appreciated, very much, the efforts that we had made to make ourselves understood. Incidentally, nearly three years on they still speak no English but, fortunately, our French has improved considerably so we have few problems. We realised very early on that one should always be prepared to have a go at speaking in French – it is very much appreciated and makes the French think that the English are perhaps quite nice after all! It's a pity that the day trippers on their booze trips to Calais don't try a bit harder – I am sure that they are the people on whom we are judged as a nation.

Back at the caravan – just two minutes' drive, sheer bliss – the pressure was off.

'Open the wine,' my wife said.

I didn't need a second bidding. In fact, I didn't even need a first. Pop, the cork was out. We felt that if we could do as well as we had done today, limited though we were, then within three years, with a lot of help and hard work, we would be fluent French speakers. Only time would tell.

The sun came out. With a glass of wine in our hands we could relax. Fortunately, we had some garden furniture in the trailer – we had our priorities right! We'd guessed (hoped) that we would be sitting out a lot, in between clearing up the dirt, dust and grime.

As usual, I could not sit still for long, and with the first glass of wine downed I pushed the stable door, or rather what remained of it, open. It squeaked and groaned, sounding a bit like me the morning after a hard day's work. In the main room there was dirt and two house martins' nests, the residents of which were most put out to be disturbed. We immediately decided that nothing major would be done until the young had flown, which, with luck, would be before the end of September. Beware of house martins and swallows – they can, and often do, hatch as many as three lots of eggs in a summer season! This, of course, was making the assumption that they were prepared to put up with us. Next year they would have to find alternative accommodation, such as that enjoyed by their relations in our adjoining barn. We were not going to be able to do much to the door, and whatever we did do, we would have to leave a gap until they finally left. But we *would* be able to repair the window, assuming that I either had the required skills or was able to acquire them!

Oh it was so difficult to know where to start, but we really felt that we had to do something – the first day of our meagre thirty was nearly over. As per usual, my wife wanted to start in six places at the same time and to finish the whole place within a month. I saw this as enthusiasm rather than as anything else, but I was trying, with difficulty, to be practical. For once I did not ponder or pontificate (as the three elder children, if they had been there, would have anticipated). I made an instant decision that I was either going to start in the main room or the smaller room, which was to be the kitchen. Because first impressions are important to me I decided that it was to be the main room first – I could not stand the sight of the window patched with galvanised iron and polythene sacks which had been tied in as well as forced into the holes. By the time I had finished that day I almost wished that I had never started. The bottom part of the window frame on one side was totally missing, as were the bottom two panes of glass and the next three pieces of wood. The two horizontals and the vertical were all rotten. Oh dear – what a way to start! Ah well, there was no going back, as my wife eagerly reminded me. What on earth was I doing? Attempting the impossible, I felt.

'Yes, you have got to do it today,' said my daughter. 'You have to keep the burglars out!'

My only consolation at this time was that since I'd removed the galvanised sheets and the polythene sacks, the room was getting lighter.

It may be fortunate, it may be not, but I am a hoarder – something to which my wife will testify. I never throw anything away, just in case it might be useful – except bent nails. My wife's uncle (a retired GP) wouldn't even throw those away, he would carefully straighten them. It just goes to show what a miserly background I have! However, it comes in useful.

Before leaving England I had placed some sheets of glass of varying sizes in the trailer and also an assortment of bits of wood varying from beading to two inches by one inch. Reassured by this, I did feel that by the end of the day the window would be weatherproof! When I got the bits together I was not so sure. I began to wonder if there was anything ready-made lying around that could possibly be adapted – you never know your luck. I poked around the barns opposite but found nothing of use and the same went for the outhouse in which a magnificent bread oven was situated. But eventually I was rewarded – in the top attic I found two old window frames which were partly damaged and rotten in places but likely to provide me with sufficient bits to patch the windows downstairs. I crossed my fingers and hoped. I got them downstairs and found to my relief that I had the two horizontals and the vertical piece that I needed but not the bottom piece – this would have to be made. This was not something that I was going to be able to complete that day or at least not finish properly. Oh no, I was going to have to put the dreaded polythene back! It had not been a very good start. It was going to have to wait until tomorrow. To relax, unwind and vent my frustrations, I decided to do something different. I would clear out the kitchen, or rather the room that was to be the kitchen. I think it must have been the room where the farmer, who had not lived in Le Manoir but used it as a store, had made his wine, or at least bottled it. He had also made butter there. There was an awful lot to be moved but fortunately in my trailer-load of bits and pieces I had included a wheelbarrow – a good job too. There were four full loads, mainly of empty bottles together with the old butter vat. With all this removed, and the butter vat carefully stored for restoration, it was beginning to look more like a room. There was an open fireplace at one end, a small window at the other and a larger window in the middle. It all seemed pretty dark and dingy and at the time I could not see how I was going to improve it. I eventually did it with the help of my younger daughter's housemistress, although she knew nothing about it. Just how she helped me, well, that story comes later!

We suddenly realised that we hadn't had any lunch, nor a proper breakfast either, and it was now 5.30 p.m. We felt that although we had not achieved very much, we had done enough for the first day, and that we should eat, have a glass of wine and if we did not fall asleep, do some sensible planning. We had to get organised as my wife, in one of her weaker moments, had not only invited Pierre and his wife to dinner during the next few days, but also our elder son was expected for a couple of days, together with his wife and three of their friends. Many hands make light work, I thought, but then I remembered that they were all coming to relax, eat well and drink wine – most probably my wine! Work, apart from lifting a plate and a bottle, would not be in their itinerary. I would just have to press on, which reminded me that although we had plates and cutlery, we had no chairs to sit on (apart from garden chairs) and certainly no table. No doubt the Royal Command would soon come for me to make benches and a table suitable for ten people to sit around. I would cross that bridge as and when I came to it.

The evening was uneventful. Since it was warm and sunny we just sat outside and enjoyed the peace. We had begun to realise that the restoration was going to take us a lot longer than we had perhaps first thought! I looked up to the sky and quietly asked for an extension (to my years, that is!). I had the feeling that he was grinning at me and saying, 'You bought it – it's up to you. Don't just sit there, get on with it!'

We retired early, intent on starting at dawn. We had forgotten just how early dawn is and had certainly not reckoned on the noise of our resident owl, who was either giving us a series of welcoming calls or telling us to clear off and to leave him in peace. To this day I am not really sure which it was but it was probably the latter because since we moved in he has moved to another building close by – one not inhabited by *Homo sapiens*!

Alas, dawn came and went, and I was unceremoniously awoken by our friendly farmer's tractor right opposite the caravan. Why, oh why, once they have started these infernal machines, do they just leave them ticking over for half an hour? If it were I, I would just get it started and drive off to do whatever I had intended. I could perhaps have understood if the tractor had been an old Fordson, which needs a long warming-up period and which was difficult to start but this is a spanking new John Deere!

I was thinking about the window in the house as I dressed and drank my first of many cups of coffee. I was worried that my woodworking skills were not perhaps up to it, and I did not want it to look a bodge but I knew I had to do something. I went out of the caravan and had a close look at the window, at least what there was of it. I came to the conclusion that for it to look right, it needed the skills of a proper joiner, and that I was not. I just stood and looked, at the same time lighting one of my cigars. The only time I smoke these days is when I smoke duty-free cigars, and once my ration is gone that's it until the next trip. I will only smoke Villager Export, that is, apart from a fine Havana, but alas nobody offers me these anymore. I don't think I have had one for some seventeen years, not since one of my great friends died. Lit up, I decided to wander, yet another confirmation that I find it difficult to keep still. I went to take another look at the contents of the outbuildings. There were parts of an old cider press, some very large horseshoes that could only have belonged to a shire and various harnesses. Then, under a load of hay, which had presumably fallen through a hole in the floor of the loft above, much to my delight I discovered a couple of window frames. Admittedly they were both in some disrepair, but one of them had a bottom bar which looked as if it was the same size as the one I was missing. Removing it was easy – it more or less fell from the frame. Taking it quickly to the house I found that it was within an inch of the size that I wanted – fortunately an inch too big! A tenon saw and a hammer and chisel allowed me to make the necessary adjustments, and by the time that my wife and daughter emerged I had it more or less in position. They were both impressed. Gluing, screwing and clamping followed and by lunchtime it was completed – including the glazing. I reckoned that once it was puttied and painted it would look like the original, from a distance anyway – say twenty feet! If you are a good bodger then you can produce a result as good as most builders, the only difference being that he knows the eventual outcome when he starts whereas all I can do is hope and pray that it is going to work out and then be pleasantly surprised when it does. Please note that I do not mention the countless things which can and do go wrong – that would ruin one's image of being (apparently) successful!

My wife in the meantime had been sorting through the debris in what was to be her kitchen. I had managed to persuade her that it would be much better than using the cellar (I might still have it exclusively as a wine cellar yet, although there would be little chance of filling it!). The odd worm wriggling and slugs sliding across the floor had quickly put her off.

'I'm not going back in there again,' she muttered, 'until it's pest free.'

So she was back in the main room, poking at the fireplace and then at the partition that hid the stairs.

'The partition will have to go as a matter of urgency,' she said.

At that stage I had other ideas as I thought it might be a bit too physical. I was feeling a bit fragile, but I reckoned I would have to give in later.

It dawned on us at this stage that we had nowhere to put our rubble. That did not include the vast quantity of empty wine bottles abandoned in the kitchen. Being a reasonable environmentalist, I was going to take those to a bottle bank, assuming that I could find one.

At this stage my wife came to the rescue.

'We will build a patio,' she said, 'and any rubble will form the foundations.'

That was a useful suggestion.

After that she forgot about the removal of the partition (temporarily) and the general process of cleaning downstairs begun. When a house has been uninhabited, by humans that is, for probably the best part of three hundred years, and has just been used as a much unloved agricultural store and general dumping ground, it is difficult to know where to start. There was dust, dirt and grain everywhere, (upstairs had been used as a grain store with a tube that came down through the ceiling), and there was lots of earth on the floor. After a couple of days of sweeping, it looked just as bad – would it ever look right? It's a good job that we are optimists.

One of the main causes of the dirt was the fire. Over the years, the previous farmers had hung their hams, half pigs and other bodies inside the chimney and used it as a smokery – hence the blackness of the walls. Clearly they had not minded the dirt and grime as they had not had to live in it. It had just been another outbuilding to them – a store and an extension to their kitchen for smoking food.

Looking at the fireplace and the chimney again, I just could not work out why the whole place was so smoky. I was convinced that because of the height of the chimney and the fact that it was very straight there would have been little chance of any fire smoking and that it must have been made to smoke for curing purposes. No doubt we would find out in due course as we burnt our logs, which would have to be the size of tree trunks. It was at this stage I nearly had a problem.

My wife said, 'Why don't we put a wood-burning stove in the fireplace? That would stop all the dirt and dust.'

Ugh, I thought, but felt that I should not be too strong at this stage. I should just say nothing and hope that she forgot about it. Just imagine putting a wood-burning stove into such a magnificent fireplace, particularly when it was a replica of the one on Le Mont St Michel. At this stage I think we both felt that it was wise to be diplomatic and let the matter rest as neither of us was going to give in to the other. We are both strong characters and we knew that after nearly thirty years of marriage it was better to keep our own counsel and try again later when one felt that the other party was more amenable. It may sound like 'Games People Play' – who can say truthfully in a long marriage that this never happens – but it isn't meant to be. It's just the way we operate and the reason why we have always had a good relationship – well most of the time!

My wife looked at the walls of the room. They were nearly twelve feet high and covered some one thousand square feet. She wondered just what she could do, and how quickly (or was it even possible?). She could restore them to their former glory – these grey, very dirty walls, covered in cracked plaster. Removal of the plaster would not be difficult, but alas neither of us knew how to plaster. Somehow, I don't know why, this was one of the skills we could never master. Without making too fine a point, our efforts have always been pathetic. We have tried numerous times but have always ended up with plaster three feet deep around us and absolutely nothing on the walls! Ah well, you can't expect to be an expert at everything. I left my wife to ponder over that one whilst I, crowbar and lump hammer in hand, decided to attack the partition – using anything more delicate would have got me absolutely nowhere.

Unfortunately for me, the partition was extremely well constructed and attached very firmly to the staircase, the floor and the main roof beams by six-inch nails. However, with my daughter's assistance things gradually began to happen. The partition door came off quite easily as it was hinged to the rest of the partition, but the next three or four supporting timbers proved to be quite difficult, even with a lot of brute force. Obviously I did not want to cause any damage either to the main beam running the length of the room or to the staircase. Thank goodness both the main beam and the staircase were solid oak. There was not much chance of splintering or shattering them. If I had thought that there was any chance, then I would have been a lot more careful. I would not have relished the thought of replacing a twenty-four-foot beam, of which twenty-two feet were exposed, which was twenty inches high and sixteen inches wide, assuming that I could even have found one, nor the other supporting beams, which numbered thirty-six in all. They were only supporting the floorboards, but they were a massive nine inches by seven inches. To pay for their replacement one would have had to take out a second mortgage.

I must say that I did know that all the timbers were sound, as this was one thing that I *had* checked thoroughly before agreeing to buy. As you will realise, I did not employ a surveyor or have any structural checks carried out.

I worked on the principle that if the building had stood for the best part of nine hundred years then there was little chance of it falling down. Then I did the following three things:

(a) A visual examination of the exterior to see if the roof was sound (which it was) and if there were any major cracks in the walls which might cause a collapse at any time.

(b) The lump hammer and screwdriver/chisel test for checking walls and timbers.

(c) A check of any services to see how functional they were. This was easy because there was no mains water or drainage, and the electricity was working.

The building had passed my tests, well, more or less, on the first visit, although there was some rot at the end of one of the main beams where it entered the wall in the main room. This had been caused by rain seeping in over the centuries but it was nothing that a well-disguised concrete pillar would not only cure but also hide.

Sorry, I have digressed. I was talking about the partition. It turned out to be a much longer job than I had anticipated. This was largely because I wanted to be as careful as possible. I wanted to be able to reuse most of the wood. It was far better quality than I could hope to buy either in England or France. This is because tongued and groove timber in both England and France is largely made from soft wood, but this was hard wood.

The whole room looked so much better once it had been removed. It looked much bigger, lighter and, I felt, even more magnificent. The staircase was now fully revealed in all its glory. It was made of carved oak and was about sixteen to twenty feet in length. It was extremely dirty, with many nails embedded in it, but it was resplendent nonetheless! Now I had a problem, or a possible problem. Since I had removed the partition, the staircase had become somewhat unstable. Just how I was going to make it rigid again I was not quite sure, but that was not going to be a job for today, nor tomorrow, for that matter. It would be done when the house was more complete, that is providing it did not collapse in the meantime! I could see that it was going to be fiddly and, bearing in mind that I was going to have to do it single-handedly (it only weighed about half a ton!), I decided to prop the top end with an acrow prop. Being a belt and braces man, I also secured it with some climbing rope to one of the beams upstairs.

My wife at this stage was still cleaning. This was a task that took the best part of three weeks or more –almost to the end of our first month. She then said that she would start cementing or plastering or something. That sounded like good news as:

(a) It got me off the hook, because if I was working for her then I could not be doing anything off my own bat.

(b) I had fortunately brought the faithful electric cement mixer with me – the things that I had crammed into that box trailer!

(c) It would keep her out of my hair, that is, provided the mix was right and I was doing it fast enough.

I really am most rude about my wife! She's lovely really – well, most of the time.

I suggested at this stage that until all the loose plaster had been removed, we should perhaps not start cementing. As you already know, neither of us can plaster, so this was going to be the technique, keeping our fingers crossed that it would stick to the walls. At this stage she said we should just clear the plaster above a particular ledge, just to see how easily (or not!)it came off. The ledge was some two feet wide, six or so feet above the floor and to the left of the fireplace.

'Seems as good a place as any to start,' I said.

I had been aware of it before and thought it would be quite a good place for some of my earthenware pitchers, but that apart, it did not appear to be particularly significant. How wrong I was going to be proved to be! I don't know why I thought it, but looking at it more closely I just felt that the back wall was not as solid as it appeared and that it might be hiding something. I got a pair of steps and began to attack it (gently) with a pecking hammer. From the first blow it had a hollow ring – was this to be an entrance to a secret passage? I tapped gently and the plaster began to come away. This was exciting! I got through the plaster and embedded the point of my pecking hammer in some wood. A small door with very old iron hinges was revealed. The time had come to be more delicate. Using my hands more than the pecking hammer, I removed the remaining bits of plaster. The door was uncovered for probably the first time in centuries. It measured thirty inches by twenty inches, but what was beyond it? To where did it lead? With the aid of a screwdriver I eventually managed to prise it open. My reward was an iron grid behind the door. This was one of the original windows in the building, which had never been glazed and retained its original shutter. This caused me to look at all the other openings in the building and, lo and behold, in all of them were holes on both sides, above and below where the iron bars had been. I assumed that in the case of the doors these had been somehow removable, although I couldn't really work out quite how. I also made the assumption that these openings had been covered by shutters. It would be fascinating to know just when they had been removed and replaced by windows – sadly I doubt that I will ever know. Each day I became more and more intrigued with the house, never knowing quite what I was going to find next. We felt strongly that we would have to do everything ourselves for fear of something being destroyed because nobody else, particularly a French builder, would be interested in retaining or restoring the various facets as we would. Now all that we needed was to find the tunnel which was supposedly two kilometres in length, but that's another story.

How were we coping in the caravan you might be wondering. I think the honest answer would be 'cramped but comfortable'! Having spent so much time over the years in France in a caravan, we were used to it. Fortunately, we know our way around the supermarkets very well and find them much more interesting than their English equivalents, but more important than that is that my wife is a marvellous cook. I am sure that we eat to Michelin standard (three red stars of course!) all the time and, of course, we always have a good wine list, that is providing we have been shopping! Confirmation of my wife's culinary skills came years ago when I was running a course for senior managers at our home in the Cotswolds. Unbeknown to us, one of the managers had invited one of the main board members down to eat with us on the final evening and for the rest of the evening after the meal the aforesaid gentleman spent his time trying to persuade my wife to run the directors' dining room in London. She declined, but to this day wonders if she made the right decision – ah well!

Chapter IV

Because I have not mentioned him you might well imagine that all was quiet on the farmer front, but you would be wrong! I had another embarrassing incident, and this one could have been a disaster. As you will remember, it is my wont to come from the caravan first thing in the morning, clad in my pyjamas, to listen to the radio. I am an early riser, but not as early as our farmer friend. A few days after our arrival I was sitting there, quietly minding my own business, when my peace was shattered by a tapping on the roof. There he was smiling at me and inviting me to walk my boundary so that I would know what land was ours and obviously what was not. I climbed out of the car and he tried to shake my hand. As I went to shake it I nearly lost my somewhat ill-fitting pyjama trousers. I pulled back immediately and grabbed my pyjamas – it was much better to offend him than to appear naked in front of him, with his wife close at hand. The mind boggles. He didn't seem too wounded and off we went. I was glad that I went with him as I found that I had quite a bit more land than I had originally realised, which would make access for my old sit-on lawnmower that much easier – that is when we had got rid of the copious undergrowth.

After this event I felt I had finally learned my lesson. I make sure that I dress as soon as I get up now so that no matter who calls I will be ready for them. My wife was very embarrassed by the whole situation, whilst really I found it quite funny, in hindsight that is. As a result, when I get up she asks if I'm sure I'm properly dressed. Not something I think that I am going to forget in a hurry!

It was whilst we were not working, eating or drinking – that does not leave much of my twenty-four-hour day – that we had an unexpected visitor, one of the very few that we had in our somewhat isolated situation. We were half a mile from other people. It must have been about ten thirty at night and we were thinking about retiring to bed when we heard the noise of a vehicle approaching. It was larger than a car but smaller than a lorry, yet definitely not a tractor. I opened the caravan door not quite sure who had arrived or whom they were looking for – it couldn't possibly be us. There was a largish van, and coming from within it, a horrendous banging noise. Almost immediately, I was confronted by a behatted Frenchman who announced that he had returned our horse and complained that he had had a dickens of a job finding us. He did not wait for my reply, which was taking a long time as I was temporarily speechless (something that my wife has rarely seen!).

'All is now well,' he said as he turned to walk to the vehicle where his companion was already opening the door at the back to release this wild animal. My protestations and denials were falling on deaf ears – the local *vétérinaire* was obviously convinced that it was my horse and this was where he was going to leave it. I am not quite sure just how I managed to convince him that he was in the wrong place and that the horse was not mine, unless it was when I showed him the state of the barn – at least now he was listening to my protestations! I then explained to him in French, which was miraculously improving, that there was a riding school and stables just five kilometres away and that the owner had told me that he was awaiting the return of his horse. The riding school did exist but the conversation was a figment of my imagination. At least he was now convinced that he was in the wrong place – it was a way of getting rid of him!

He closed the van and he and his assistant, still perhaps not totally convinced, turned around and drove off. I was still not totally convinced that he would not come back, but my wife reassured me and persuaded me to have a glass of wine and go to bed and forget about it. I did as I was bid and she, as on many occasions, was proved to be right. We had peace for the rest of the night, that is apart from our neighbourhood owl who I am sure was complaining that we had moved in and had disturbed his regular supply of rodents!

The days were going by and my extended holiday was over – we had had our dinner party and my son and his wife and friends had visited. As I had anticipated, not a finger was raised in the way of physical help, but I did not mind as it gave me a chance to have a break. My wife, however, had to do all the cooking. Yes, I did manage to make a dining table. It was a sheet of chipboard, balanced on pillars of breeze-blocks and covered with a blue sheet. It looked very effective. I had made two benches from two old oak planks, carefully attached to some small uprights. They must have been reasonable as both parties of guests – yes we had also had Pierre and his wife and one of his children to dinner the week before – had asked where we had found the two old oak benches (so much for their eyesight as the uprights were made from some rather scruffy three-by-two softwood). Or were they just being kind? I don't mind either way, as the benches served their purpose and did not collapse.

Some days we felt that we had achieved a lot, whilst on others we felt that we had achieved very little. On the days that we felt fulfilled, or at least partially fulfilled, we would reflect that although we had achieved a lot, because of the immensity of the task it could possibly take us another twenty years, and that was without looking at the barns, unless I retired and we lived in France permanently. This was very tempting but not practical as yet. I looked upwards, as I often do and said, 'How about an extension?' but alas there was no reply.

But I almost felt somebody saying, 'You have had more than your fair share already – just get on with it and work a bit harder.' Perhaps whoever said it was right, not that I am one to stand and stare for long. There is no peace for the wicked – perhaps I should try not to be so wicked!

At this stage I remembered what various grannies, mothers, maiden aunts, mothers-in-law and my beloved godmother had said to me – the latter had been a lovely lady, very much larger than life with a booming voice, who had driven a bubble car down the middle of the road, accompanied by an oversized poodle called Johnny. Although unmarried, she had been very much a woman of the world. She had claimed to be a love child of Edward the seventh, when he had been Prince of Wales – who knows. Her final claim to fame, which I found very useful in my teens, was that she had been a major in the Royal Corps of Transport (the

RASC) and was an expert mechanic. Sorry, you are waiting to hear just what they said:

(a) Nothing is ever as bad as it seems.

(b) Only cowards give in!

(c) It's amazing what you can achieve with a little effort.

(d) Nothing is impossible.

(e) Every little helps.

(f) Nothing comes from nothing.

And finally, 'Anything worthwhile is well worth waiting for.' I don't know if I really go for any of these sayings in a particularly big way, but if I had to choose just one of them, then I suppose that I would go for the second one. Abide by that and I reckon that you should be able to achieve anything, adding to it my own favourite – 'The impossible never happens.'

We courageously struggled(?), persisted(?) forwards. There is always light at the end of the tunnel (somewhere!), assuming that some blighter has not blocked it up and if you do a lot today, there is either a bit less to do tomorrow or the closer you are to the end of the project. It's amazing how you can manage to convince yourself!

No chapter would be complete, at least in these early stages, without some reference to Pierre. The night of the dinner party arrived. Although it was still August, it got quite cold in the late evening so I decided to take the plunge and light a fire, keeping my fingers crossed that it would not smoke – it would be too late to change my mind once it was lit. There was no grate or basket of any description, just a slightly raised (about six inches) hearth. In true Boy-Scout tradition I collected lots of small twigs and some larger branches and then looked around for larger bits of wood. There were plenty. I am pleased to say it lit with the first match – that proved I had earned my firelighter's badge many, many years ago. Surprise, surprise the smoke was going straight up the chimney. In a relatively short time we had a warm fire – one could not call it cosy as the room is far too big for that description.

As you can well imagine, my wife was horrendously busy in the caravan preparing a five-course meal fit for royalty – it was alas going to be a long time before she got a proper kitchen. I was keeping well out of the way doing mundane things like tidying up, laying the table and making sure that there were enough glasses and also something to put in them. I had a reasonable stock of wine but nothing particularly exotic, just some rather nice Côte de Blaye white and some Cru Bourgeois Médoc from an unknown chateau – certainly one that I had never heard of. So far so good, and with that they arrived. Pierre was wearing a suit, and I felt tatty as I was still in more or less what were my working clothes – I had had no time to change. Then I had a pleasant surprise – it was Pierre who was armed with the Médoc. He looked around the lounge suggesting that it was coming on well, and indicated parts of the structure that might fall down. There is nothing like building up one's confidence! Then he added, 'What you need is a proper builder to sort it out.' So this was the ploy – he wanted some more work. I am sorry to say that he was going to be disappointed.

With the wine flowing and the fire roaring it looked as if it was going to be a good evening. Pierre was not as busy as he would have liked to be.

'Too many indecisive Brits,' he was complaining. 'They don't know what they want, and when you do show them something that is perfect for them, they can't make a decision and scuttle back to England.'

Perhaps it is Pierre's selling techniques that are at fault.

The meal itself was a huge success. I don't know how my wife can do it all in the cramped space of the caravan. And although I say it myself I did make some superb coffee, ground and in a cafetière, of course. This was accompanied by Calvados and a little more red wine. Pierre had acquired a boat very recently. It was a thirty footer of a class unknown to me – I'm better on dinghies and other small craft. He was trying to persuade my wife to go on a cruise with him to Guernsey. Much to her disgust (I think, but cannot be totally sure!), I said that it was all right by me, but she was saved by the bell – this planned trip was the week after we returned to England.

The evening came to an end, a very pleasant one, and then I discovered that my daughter had invited their daughter to stay the night. Oh dear, it's not very easy to get four people into a two-berth caravan, at least not without the aid of a shoehorn! It was all organised so no protestations coming from me could change this. Pierre and his wife departed, leaving me to wonder just where I was going to sleep. If it was in the caravan, then I would have to be standing up, so that was out. The other choices were the car or on a camp bed in the vast lounge. I didn't really fancy either but plumped for the house, eerie though I might well find it. Surprisingly enough, I dropped off to sleep very quickly, only to be startled some hours later by a scuffling, scraping noise by the fire. What could it be? I dived for my torch, which naturally enough I then knocked over, and hurriedly turned it on. When I had retrieved it and turned it on, I caught sight of a rather mangy, but large cat – or was it? It had a reddish skin colour. I yelled at it and it disappeared. It had obviously been searching for scraps from our meal, and to this day I have never seen it since and really cannot be sure of just what it was. Appropriately, for the rest of the night I catnapped, making the clear decision that in no way was I sleeping in the house until it was cat-and-other-animal-proof. It wasn't that I was frightened in any way – I just did not feel comfortable!

One night in there was enough for me at the moment, so at lunchtime we returned the aforesaid daughter to Pierre and his wife. I was not doing that again in a hurry.

Now, alas, it was time to pack as soon our month would be up and we would be back to reality. How did we feel? I suppose 'muddled' is the best description, knowing that we had to go back and not wanting to, but worst of all was not knowing exactly when we could get back. It would have to be at half-term, and that was almost six weeks away.

Saturday came all too soon – alas, *les grandes vacances terminent* – and it was back to *Angleterre* with an empty trailer in tow.

Chapter V

The next few weeks passed by very quickly. There was so much catching up to do, not only with work but with domestic matters as well, not least of all bringing the garden back under control. Thank goodness we are not lawn lovers, so there was no grass to be cut, but there was an awful lot of weeding, transplanting and taking of last-minute cuttings, which we hoped to goodness would take before the frosts set in. We also had to decide just when we were going to bring the geraniums and other non-hardy plants in – most difficult of all was where we were going to store them. Most window sills in our house spent six months of the year covered in geraniums, and even though we were very careful, we still managed to lose more than half of them. But as usual it did not stop us from trying. As I said before, we are born optimists, but this year it was very important as many of the surviving plants were to be taken to France in the spring. Our problem is that every time we move, in England that is, we move further north, but always manage to forget that (a) the winter is probably going to be longer and (b) it is probably going to be a lot colder. We are hoping that this will be far less of a problem when we are permanently in France. Certainly we can be assured of warmer and longer summers, but I am not too sure about the winters.

About two weeks after we got back, we sat down one evening and opened a rather nice bottle of Paulliac (one of the best tasting Médoc wines and certainly value for money), intent on talking about Le Manoir and just what we were going to do to it next. Obviously it had been on our minds ever since we had got back, but we simply had not had sufficient time to sit and talk about it, and for me to produce my 'ideas book' and my wife to produce her drawings. How did we feel? We were very happy with our purchase, but we still felt that perhaps we had been mad to take on such an undertaking. We were most definitely pleased with the progress to date, but wished that we had managed an awful lot more. Would we be able to move into the house within twelve months? It was highly doubtful, I felt. My wife, however, felt that we probably could. I thought of saying, 'Yes, a frame tent in the main room,' but I decided to be charitable and said, 'We'll have a go.' Yes, but what were we going to do when we visited it for half-term? Because of the way that I was working we were actually going to be able to manage six days in France, and we were determined that this was not going to be wasted. In a way I felt that we ought to do something outside before the winter came, whenever that was going to be. I felt that starting on the patio was a must, if only to hide all the rubble that we had dumped and were continuing to dump. At the same time I thought we should work out just where we were going to plant our hedges of *cypress lawsawni* both around the grounds and the house. It would be much easier, I felt, to buy them in France than to hump them over in the trailer – this was very quickly confirmed when I found out just how many my wife wanted!

'How many do you need,' I said casually to my wife.

'Oh around one hundred to one hundred and twenty,' she said.

'How many,' I shrieked.

Well, if that was the case I most certainly would not be taking that little lot over from England, as it would more than fill the trailer, unless I bought little six-inch plants. But I knew that my wife would not be fobbed off with that one.

'Most interesting,' I said, and made an attempt to change the subject and talk about a topic that would prove to be less expensive, at least in the short term.

I suggested that as she was so good at drystone walling – no really, she is, probably because she was deprived of building bricks when she was a child – she should begin building a drystone wall around where my mound of rubble was growing. I would provide her with lots of suitable stone and more rubble, flatten it out, put down a damp proof course and before she knew it she would have a patio. I knew an instant wife would like an instant patio! I knew that she would warm to this, but before she got too carried away, I asked what sort of chippings she would like to have on it. I knew that she would have preferred slabs but not only are these quite difficult to lay completely flat – thank you for your confidence, madame – but they are also expensive! If you think I sound like a scrooge, you should see my nose! She decided on grey/granite chippings – not beyond my skill for laying and also within my budget! I didn't ask what she wanted me to do inside after that, as I knew the list would prove too unending and difficult to prioritise.

So that was the end of a good and fruitful evening of discussion but alas the bottle of Paulliac had been well and truly drained, although we'd been careful to leave the sediment in the bottom. No more of that until we returned to France – I was not paying fancy English prices! There was, however, a reasonable supply of other drinkable, but humbler, wines in my rack – alas I do not possess a cellar in England at the present time. I have some rather nice Côte de Blaye, both red and white, some Côte de Bourg, some Haut Médoc and some Fronsac. The latter is a great favourite of my wife's after a memorable visit to a chateau there that we had nearly twenty years ago, but that's another story!

On second thoughts, I think that I had better tell it as it is really quite funny. In the mid- and late seventies we used to take the caravan – my wife and I and the three children – to stay on the Arcachon Basin, long before the Brits ever found it and whilst it was still pollution-free. Each year we would meet up with a couple of families with children of similar ages to ours. It was marvellous. Sometimes my wife and the children would spend the whole of the summer holidays there whilst the breadwinner flew back and forth, each time returning with loads of baked beans and other English goodies (in their eyes) for the children. Why isn't life like this any more? I blame the galloping major, the one who followed after the iron lady! Anyway, back to the story. Each summer the owner of the campsite would allow the proprietor of a vineyard in the Bordeaux region (no doubt in exchange for a couple of cases, who knows) to come to the campsite for a wine tasting. You could also purchase the wine and, if you felt so inclined, buy a ticket for a coach trip to that particular vineyard. We tasted some Fronsac and liked its rather earthy flavour – it was much nicer for our palates than the neighbouring St Émilion. We had never heard of it and doubted if many other Brits had, apart from Berry Bros and Rudd

(Yapp had probably tasted it but they were not really in full swing then). And undoubtedly John Avery knew where it was and where it came from. Anyway, we decided to join the coach trip and duly paid our fifty francs, which was to cover the cost of the trip plus yet another tasting. I wonder if anybody has ever realised just how much you can (and do) consume at a French wine tasting – it had to be a minimum of a bottle and a half each!

It was very interesting to visit the area where Fronsac is produced – it is quite a small area just beyond Mérignac. It appears to be fairly intensively grown and I would imagine that the land supports very little apart from grapevines. We were shown how the grapes were grown and it was explained to us that they were restricted, quite severely, with regard to the number of vines that they had, where they were grown and why. We were talked through at length the harvesting, winemaking and maturing process. Finally, we were told that they always produced good wine but that there were some years when it was very much better than others! It was all very interesting, but we really wanted to begin the tasting. Fortunately we did not have long to wait! We were ushered, all fifty of us, forty-four French and just six Brits (children to be left outside!), into a long shed adjoining the wine vats and bottling plant. It was different from the usual sort of tasting, certainly those of the grand chateaux of the Médoc (the latter certainly worth a visit even though you do not intend buying any!), mainly because each time you had a taste you had half a glassful and were not expected to spit it out after tasting – if you were I never saw the offending receptacle in which you're supposed to spit. I can't remember hearing any complaints!

We tasted the previous year's wine and the two before that, and although we were shown the bottles of some of the earlier vintages and told how wonderful they were, we were not allowed the joy of tasting them – no, not even a thimbleful. However, the French appeared to feel that it was all 'good value' and were freely purchasing their cases. This must have impressed the proprietor, because he then said that as we were all such lovely people, he would open a barrel (probably the size of a firkin – four and half gallons to the uninitiated) of a particular five-year-old wine that he felt we would all love. This of course was a chance for him to sell some wine that was more expensive than the wine that we had already purchased. Surprise, surprise – the ploy worked!

It was at this stage that the funny incident happened. My wife needed the loo and, not being a lover of the hole in the ground which much of the French still seemed happy with twenty years ago – how things have changed – she had no option but to find it. She went in quickly but was not fast enough getting out. She pressed the lever to flush it, not realising that the hose was attached to the wall, with the functional end immediately above her. She screamed, as per normal, and came out dripping wet, but otherwise none the worse for wear! It's a good job that she had had a couple of glasses of wine. She vowed then that she would never use another French loo again. This has not happened, but she very clearly meant it at the time.

We worked our way through the barrel fairly rapidly, which I reckon worked out on average at about three glasses each, five each for the greedy and one for the more abstemious – not that I saw many of those around! How many extra cases he sold I just don't know, but judging from his joyous farewell it must have been worth his while. I certainly do not remember the journey back to the Arcachon basin, but I do remember the sore head the next morning!

The weeks went by quickly and we prepared ourselves for our return to France. The passages were booked and we anticipated that we would arrive just after breakfast on Saturday morning – this was one advantage of being just two hours from the port. For a change, the journey went very smoothly. Even the M6 seemed prepared for us and did not produce any nasty jams around Birmingham, which it is prone to do. It was plain sailing, and we arrived at Portsmouth with more than an hour to spare. This was most unusual for us as we normally arrive just as they are about to close the bow doors and on many occasions we have been the last vehicle on board. This can be quite useful because it means that you are one of the first vehicles off the following morning.

There was plenty of time for changing my money this time. I don't know where you change your money – whether you change it at the bank, bring traveller's cheques or Eurocheques. We have tried the lot and reckon the best thing is to change your money at the exchange in the port, right in front of where you park before being called for boarding. Not only do you get a better exchange rate, but also there is no commission. This is ideal if you are changing small sums of money, and on the way back the same applies and they take small coins as well. On a sum of two hundred pounds you can reckon on being fifty francs better off than you would be if you'd used the 'other exchange' or the on-board rate – why throw money away!

We were fairly heavily laden this time. It must have been the cheap cement that I had put in the boot, or was it, at last, the suspension beginning to fail! I had a bet with my wife that as we went through customs we'd get stopped for a vehicle check. If you believe that there is totally free passage now that we are in the EEC then forget it. If you are travelling on your own, particularly from France to England, then you stand a ninety per cent chance of being stopped so make sure that you have your story ready! I won. We got pulled into a separate bay. They closed the doors behind us, and then asked us, 'What is in the vehicle? Did you load it yourself and did you leave it unattended at any time?' They then slid things underneath (cameras?), I suppose searching for drugs, etc. In minutes we were back with our fellow travellers who had not been treated with the same suspicion as ourselves. They eyed us curiously, almost with suspicion! We had at least a warm welcome aboard the *Pride of Portsmouth*. It's our favourite craft, probably because we know all the crew. We were rewarded with a calm crossing without too much on-board noise.

We were up at 5.45 a.m. and off the boat by 7 a.m. My wife told me it was 6 a.m. as her biological clock does not adjust as easily as mine. As usual we were on our way very quickly, with no sign of any passport control or customs, although this was to change! We moved very quickly through Le Havre, using the underpasses, and we were on our way to the Pont de Tancerville. How we longed for the Pont de Normandie to be completed – we hoped it would be the following spring (this would cut thirty minutes off our journey). It was not that the road is bad, but just that one's time is limited and one wants to make use of every single minute of it.

There were queues of lorries on the approach to Tancerville but I noted that the outside lane was free, which led to the *rapide* toll booth. These are designed just for cars, accepting exact money only, but in any assortment of coins. We were up and away in seconds.

'Next stop, the house,' I said, with hope!

We went via the scenic route through Pont l'Evêque, Lisieux and very close to Camembert, and all we had to eat was some French bread, quickly grabbed as we passed through Lisieux. Once through Lisieux we saw hardly a car in either direction – why are French roads so quiet? I suppose it is because France is four times the size of England but with more or less the same population, but even allowing for this, I just always expect to see more cars.

In under two hours we were in La Ferté Macé – less than fifteen minutes from Le Manoir. Although it was Sunday, we week. The shop was not a supermarket or a hypermarket – it was what I call an 'in-between' shop, somewhere that stocks everything at very competitive prices. This particular one, because it opens on Sundays, is closed on Mondays! We had read in the papers (and we are talking about 1994) and also heard from people who we met in France that France was expensive. I don't know where they do their shopping as it is not what we find. Things such as cheese, wine, beer, ham and prepared meats etc. are most definitely cheaper, although meat itself tends to be more expensive. You also get a much better choice, and if this means you have to pay a premium then in my mind it is well worth the premium. It will be Beaujolais Nouveau in less than a month, so as is customary all over France, they have a wine fair prior to it. Whether this is just to get people in the wine-drinking mood, or whether it is to get rid of surplus stocks – or a combination of them both – I do not know, but by the loaded trolleys that are coming out, and this is on a Sunday, then it certainly appears to have done the trick. Please note that the small supermarkets that open on Sunday mornings are closed all day on Monday!

Whilst wandering around, I espied, tucked away and not on any special display, some 1994 wine. We were still in 1994 and still a month off Nouveau day. Closer examination revealed that it was a Primeur from the Côte d'Or (around the Carcasson area, south of Bordeaux), and at nine francs eighty centimes it had got to be worth sampling. Could it be really good? Should I go to the car and sample it? I thought. No, not at nine o'clock in the morning. It could be good, but it could be dreadful. Decisions, decisions. My deceased great aunt solved it for me, or the vibrations that she was giving me. It is because of her that I always carry a corkscrew with me (along with a bottle opener). On my eighteenth birthday she gave me a little extra present – a corkscrew that folded into itself – with these kind words: 'Carry it with you always. You never know when you might meet someone with a bottle of wine who says he would share it with you if he had a corkscrew – you can call his bluff!' As a result it has been my constant companion for nearly forty years, but I have found few friends with unopened bottles – most of my friends only have empty ones! However where it does clearly come in useful is what I shall relate to you now. Clearly the only way to find out if something is drinkable is to taste it. So I did, as I have done on many occasions particularly when we used to disappear to Bordeaux. I disappeared through the cash desk with two bottles, a bottle of the Primeur and a bottle of Côte de Beaune, so that I could have something of similar body to compare it with. Both were very nice. I was positively reluctant to go back into the mini-market even though it was barely nine o'clock in the morning. Still, I did not want to get into the French habit of drinking early in the morning. I am still amazed by how busy some of the bars are as soon as they open at seven o'clock in the morning. Pickled by breakfast – it's amazing that they get anything done!

As I reappeared in the mini-market, none the worse for my little excursion, my wife enquired as to the quality, and on hearing my comments, she looked forward to her first taste. I did not buy any more Côte de Beaune as I knew that there would be plenty of that available – just half a dozen bottles of the Primeur. The rest of the shopping was done – with lots of lovely cheese, hot croissants, pâté and fresh vegetables we were on our way to Le Manoir – off to peace and tranquillity.

Chapter VI

It was just how we had left it – at least that was how it appeared. There was no noise, apart from the birds. There was a little robin hopping around and chirping and a chaffinch right up on the top chimney, singing away continuously as if his life depended upon it. It was music to the ears. Since it was the end of October the swallows would almost definitely be at the start of their long journey to South Africa. There was certainly enough time to remove the offending nests from within the Le Manoir. They could have the barn opposite for another year. We would have to make sure that there were no gaps big enough in the roof, windows or walls for them to get through when April came. We knew from previous experiences in old houses that they could fly through incredibly small holes/gaps – surely they must be equipped with radar!

We unlocked the lower door, the cellar door. I don't know why we had bothered to lock it as we had only propped the main door closed! I suppose once you own something you feel that because it is yours, you should protect it – not that there was a lot to protect, other than the fireplaces. Yes, as we had expected all the birds had flown from the two nests in the main room and the four in the cellar were also vacant. But there were an awful lot of droppings underneath all of them – we could certainly do without that next year, even though I am fond of swallows! They would have to find room with their cousins in the barn opposite, I thought, as I had suggested earlier, that is making the assumption that they had all survived the twelve-thousand-mile round trip.

The whole place looked vast and deserted but had an air of peace about it. Still, there was no time to stand and stare – there was work to be done and initially it was outside, not inside! I had brought a roll of damp-proof material on the roof-rack and this was quickly unloaded together with the bags of cement from the boot. I felt relieved that I had an electric cement mixer rather than a petrol one – there was no problem in getting it started. It was ages since I had last mixed cement or concrete – was it 3:5:1, or 3:7:1 or just what was it? There was no time to ponder on that. When it came to crunch time it would come back to me, I thought, hopefully. In the fields surrounding the house there was plenty of good stone which had been dug up by endless ploughing and within a couple of hours I had collected and delivered nearly a dozen wheelbarrow loads – that was more than enough to get my wife started on her drystone wall. That would keep her going for at least the rest of the day whilst I found some more rubble to dump and visited the local builders' merchant to see what he had in the way of chippings. Enough of the minutiae! The stone wall in its entirety grew rapidly. It was about eighteen inches high and enclosed an area fifteen feet by twenty-five feet. She finished much faster than I infilled it and I was still struggling two days later. The big problem was that I was not allowed to infill with any stone. That was a valuable commodity I was told, and only to be used for wall building. But rubble was getting harder to find as I had not been doing any demolition work. In the interludes between doing this I collected sixteen sacks of chippings, measured and paid by the shovelful – one franc a shovel, ten francs a sack! We unrolled the damp-proof material and laid it down to prevent the weeds appearing and the chippings disappearing. Another hour and all the chippings were on the damp proof course and raked over. It looked as if it had always been there – well, almost. But it certainly looked a lot tidier!

I don't know why, but my wife suddenly said that she wished we had some visitors. As she spoke we heard the noise of a vehicle coming up our road. Who could it be? Alas, it was nobody exciting – just the man from EDF, Electricité de France. He had just come to read the meter and also to check what supply we were on. He managed to weave his way around all our bits and pieces in the cellar, eventually reaching the 'kitchen'. We were on just a ten-kilowatt supply, something that I already knew, but I wanted it bumped up to thirty. He said that he could increase it to fifteen but if I wanted it increased to thirty I would have to have my wiring checked. I didn't fancy that. It was not that my wiring would not be up to scratch, but the fact that I wanted to mix both English and continental fittings and sockets. So I settled for fifteen. There was silence again when he disappeared and no more excitement until the postman arrived to deliver our weekly ration of brochures from all the neighbouring hypermarkets, each trying to seduce us with their wares and each trying to outdo the others. Nonetheless we found them very useful as they not only gave you an idea as to what they stocked but also a good idea of their prices. It was a pity we had done our shopping on our arrival – a brief read suggested that there were some bargains. But I still believe in the old adage that says you get what you pay for!

There was the sound of another car. Who could it be this time? It was a French car followed by a British car – time for a sharp exit. We were in Mayenne avoiding the Brits, unless they were friends that is, and we haven't got a lot of those! The farmhouse opposite, plus a huge barn, was also for sale – they had obviously come to look at that. Looking at them, we reckoned that they probably did not have the nouse to do the conversion themselves, so we reckoned we wouldn't see them again. We were proved right, not only with them but also with about half a dozen others who visited it over the next six months. Perhaps when we had finished our current project we would buy it if, come the Millennium, it were still for sale. We noticed that each time someone was shown over it, they turned the lights on. Funny, I thought, I could not see any evidence of any power cables. It was strange. Then I thought of the thick cable that went from our supply, out through the wall, along the side of the lean-to and disappeared into the ground. I had already asked the farmer where it went and he had just shrugged his shoulders as if to say that it had been to do with the old farm and was now redundant. I now started to wonder. I decided to turn our supply off and disconnect the cable, as after all it was not doing anything for me, and then wait for the next lot of visitors opposite. We didn't have to wait long – the next lot came, accompanied by an English agent. The lights did not work and he came over to me and asked me if we had a power supply. I said yes.

'Funny,' he said, 'the lights in the farm don't work.'

The *notaire* had told him that there was a power supply. Well, yes, there had been, and I was paying for it! Thank goodness I had ascertained this at this stage! What I still do not know is whether or not my friendly farmer genuinely did not know or whether he was taking me for a ride. I don't suppose that I shall ever know, but it will certainly cause me to be careful. It reminds me of one of our friends who bought a French property and on seeing a tap over a sink assumed that it was on mains water. But the tap was only for show – let the buyer beware! I should have been more suspicious as we had been told that there was water to our property but after the purchase it turned out that there wasn't – only to the neighbouring barn. How we got connected to mains water is another story but that comes later in the book!

Back to the farmhouse which we thought would never sell – we were right. But what would the farmer do next? We had a feeling that he might try and rent it. We thought that there was not much chance of that, but how wrong we were going to be proved to be. Over the next twelve months, various Brits – interestingly, none of them had any children – visited the barns, but nothing happened. Then it all went quiet.

Back to what we were doing. The patio, more or less finished now, had its garden furniture on it and really looked quite presentable. They were nothing garish, just a small cast-iron table and four chairs. Next year, no doubt it would be covered in geraniums. This year, because we had arrived so late, we had not bothered with any plants, although interestingly we had noticed that even though we were almost into November, most houses around still had their window boxes out with pots of hanging geraniums in them, still in full flower. I wondered if they brought them in or just left them until the first frost and started again the next year.

The man from EDF having been, and the fact that I still had an electrical supply, caused me to think that perhaps I should now begin to remove some of the frayed cable, if only to prevent us from getting electric shocks every time we touched the switch. I disconnected the supply and the cable disintegrated – at least it did not take long to remove! I did not want to do anything ambitious at this stage. I just put in a simple ring-lighting circuit downstairs, with three lights, but I left sufficient cable so that it could be tapped into on an as-and-when basis, and just one spur for power. This was not my first adventure into wiring here. The first day that we arrived I had run a spur to the caravan, which was already properly wired and protected by an isolation switch. I wasn't in the mood for finicky wiring – one of the problems when your eyes begin to fail. It would have to be done sometime, but most certainly not today!

It was one of those days when I was finding it difficult to settle to anything. I think it must have been the realisation of the enormity of the task that we had undertaken. We were trying to decide (a) if we really were normal and (b) just what we should do next. I just couldn't decide and ended too much of the philosophising. Whatever we did it didn't really matter as it was one less task to do later. Neither my wife or daughter seemed to be affected in this way and were happily busying themselves. It must be just my problem – I can't keep still for more than five minutes.

I suddenly realised that nearly an hour had gone by and there was silence from the lounge, in fact silence everywhere. What had happened to my wife? Was progress being made with regard to the walls or had she abandoned it. Dare I look? Yes, there she was –she was on her knees, with her hand in a bucket of cement (enclosed in a rubber glove, I must add). She had tried using a trowel but my mix kept falling off. Was it my mix or her technique. It was difficult to tell, but I suspect it was the former. It had to be because she had removed all the old plaster, then dampened it down. It should have worked, but it hadn't. In desperation she had decided to use her gloved hand and, to her amazement, it was working. It gave the surface a roughened look and this was what she was really after – a smooth finish would have looked totally wrong. The bad news was that it was very slow progress – how right we were. It took nearly a year to complete. This was not bad considering our infrequent visits, and it also included the treatment of the ceiling beams and the painting of the ceiling and our newly cemented walls. We used more than two hundred and fifty litres of Crepi at a cost of about a hundred pounds. If only we had realised at that stage that Crepi is watered-down Artex – how much easier our job would have been! It would have been so much easier to adjust the mix. Alas, we did not, but it will be a lot easier if we ever have to do it again, and no doubt we will.

I don't want you to think that we spent all our time working, that we never went out and that we lived in total isolation. We didn't, well at least only for some of the time. Unbeknown to us, we were being fairly continuously monitored by a little old French lady. She was dying to talk to us, but she did not know quite how to start the conversation. So all was not as quiet around us as we had first thought. Meeting her and her husband comes later though, as now there was more excitement!

There is, just around the corner from Le Manoir, a neatly restored cottage, or rather a row of cottages, owned by some Parisians whom we rarely saw. They would just escape there for a week or so in the summer. They were very friendly and said that we could use their shower and water supply etc., both when they were there and when they were not. I think that they must have been through all the building works that we were attempting but had probably had it done for them. But they still realised the inconveniences and hardships one goes through before the project is completed. We were there for our second summer – ten days in France followed by two weeks in England and then back again for a further two weeks. There was so much to do, and so little time. We were finding it rather difficult to concentrate as my wife had very recently lost her mother, so it was good that the Parisians were around. It was so nice to hear children enjoying themselves and to be surrounded by almost continuous laughter – something we had rarely heard in England. We were sorry when they returned to Paris in mid-August.

Perhaps a day, or possibly two, after their return, I noticed a large transit van parked outside the gates of their house early one morning and all the furniture on the lawn. What a pity, I thought, they are moving. It was about 8.30 a.m., just as I was on my way to pick up the hot baguettes. There was a choice of *longue* or *normal* and I always chose the former as they were slightly thinner and tasted absolutely delicious if they were split down the middle, then well buttered and stuffed with Emmental. On my way back, just a mere ten minutes later, I caught sight of the driver of the transit van. He was moustached, with greasy grey hair and smoking a *Gauloise*. I don't know why, but I just did not like the look of him. He looked a bit shifty, not the sort of person that I would have thought the Parisians would either be related to or have anything to do with. At the house I related all this to my wife, who suggested that because of my feelings I should go back and investigate. I did, but I was too late. He had clearly finished his business, or had not liked the look of me, and was disappearing around the corner in the direction of the main road. Fortunately I was able to see a part of his registration number, a '93', which indicated that he was from Paris. That was the end of that, I thought, but as I turned to walk back to the house I noticed that the furniture was still in the garden and that it had very clearly been thrown there rather than placed. Was he going to come back, or was there something going on that needed further investigation? I decided that it was the latter. I opened the side gate, the main gate being locked and found that the glass in the front door, immediately above the lock, had been smashed. Someone had broken in. On the kitchen table, clearly visible, was a half-eaten baguette and the remains of a bottle of white wine. Our moustached friend was clearly nothing to do with the Parisian family but was a burglar. He had obviously not been aware that there was anyone living around the corner and had thought that our little hamlet was deserted. In addition, I found something at the time which, although I am not superstitious (well, not actively!), sent a bit of a shiver down my spine. There was some white paint recently daubed on the ground outside the house – was it a 'Y' or an 'H' or what was it? Or was it nothing significant at all? Clearly I had to do something, and quickly, but this was not easy because at the time we were not on the telephone and I didn't want to be far from the scene just in case anything else happened. Fortunately there was a craftsman (they love to be addressed as artisans!) working on a barn less than a kilometre away so I called on him and explained that I thought that a burglary might have taken place. I asked if he could possibly contact the local gendarme. He was very pleased to help and off he went. When I got back I suddenly realised that I was going to have to make a statement to the *gendarme* so I set about writing something out. At this stage I didn't think that I would be able to speak clearly and fluently without written assistance. Fortunately, time was on my side as the *gendarme* was some three hours in coming. I had plenty of time to write, and rewrite, my statement. The more I thought about it, the more puzzled I became. What sort of burglar would scatter furniture, chairs, cushions etc. all over the grass.

Surely they would be more methodical than this. Was it something else? But if it *was* something else, just what was going on? Was it perhaps an '*affaire domestique*'?

The *gendarme* duly arrived in his large blue van. I never seem to see many police cars in France, although clearly they have them. One also has to remember that the *Gendarme Nationale* and the police are two separate organisations. My homework paid off – I was able to give a clear description of everything that I had seen. At this stage we all went through the gate into the garden and, after examining the lock, the senior of the two *gendarmes* decided that, rare though it was in this area, it had been a burglary. I volunteered that perhaps it hadn't been, and it had been an *affaire domestique*, but he was not taken with that idea and suggested that the reason he thought it was a burglary was that the locals did not like the Parisians invading their area. I wasn't convinced by his argument though. He asked me if I knew the owners' name and address, which unfortunately I did not. He looked at the situation once more, thanked me for reporting what I had seen, and away he went.

The day went by and we resumed what we had been doing. I can't remember for the life of me exactly *what* we were doing but no doubt in all probability I was humping water, sand and cement to the cement mixer and mixing wheelbarrow-load after wheelbarrow-load of cement for my beloved, whilst in between doing a bit of wiring, plasterboarding or something equally exciting. This was all in pursuit of finishing our project, which all our visitors were saying was progressing at a rapid rate. We, working on it all the time, were not quite so sure. Just before dusk the *gendarme* reappeared. He had managed to contact the owners and they would be coming down in a couple of days to sort things out. He also said that they had now established that it had not been a burglary but an *affaire domestique*, and that my description of the greasy, grey, Gauloise-smoking Frenchman had helped them confirm this.

Our peace and quiet returned. Our constant complaint that nothing ever happened at Le Manoir had been proved wrong yet again! Just what was going to happen next? It's funny, isn't it, how some people go through life and nothing seems to happen to them, let alone anything interesting, and yet with others things happen all the time! They almost seem to attract things. We most definitely fall into the latter category!

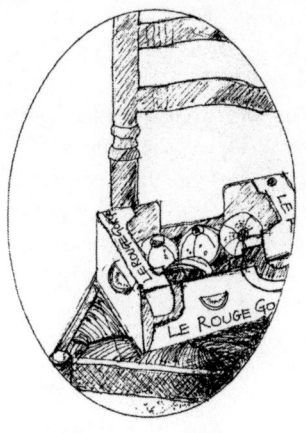

Chapter VII

With the property came a nicely fenced kitchen garden of about a quarter of an acre. That would make many people cringe, particularly as it was overgrown, but not us. In fact, both my wife and I are quite keen on gardening when we have the time – mine is of the culinary variety, my wife's more of the ornamental variety. When we first got married and I was back at university we survived because of the garden. Not only did it provide all our fruit and vegetable needs, but we also grew strawberries and raspberries on a semi-commercial basis, picking up as much as twenty pounds a day. We delivered to the local hotels. There were a large number of strawberry plants, all very weed-encroached, in our new garden – a real blast from the past. They were most unlikely to produce a reasonable crop as even though there were literally hundreds of plants, they were too overcrowded. All this would be sorted out in due time – perhaps next year but if one is being realistic then 1999 should be the target, by which time hopefully the house will have become liveable in – one that we have already missed!

One very interesting thing in the vegetable garden was the grapevine, which was growing on the back of the barn. It was some forty feet in length and looked as if it might have been planted by the monks hundreds of years ago. It looked as if it had remained untouched for a very long time, but it appeared to be healthy nonetheless. Since my knowledge of vine culture is minimal, that was the way that it was going to stay. Because of our infrequent visits the Autumn before, I think the birds had virtually eaten the whole crop but from now on things would be different. You never know, one of these days we might even end up getting a gallon or two of Chateau Le Manoir, although I have been totally forbidden from treading them. I won't go into the reasons – you can use your own vivid imagination!

Oh for a forty-eight hour day! It would be absolute bliss. So much more could be achieved, with even a little more time for relaxing. Patience is one of those virtues of which I seem to have a major deficiency. It must be a deficit from birth, so I doubt if I will change now. In addition to this I have another problem (at this stage my wife would probably suggest that I was not telling the whole truth, as I have many, many problems!), and that is that whilst I like to see things totally finished, personally I hate doing the last ten per cent. As a result I am known by the family (affectionately, I hope!) as Mr Ninety Per Cent. I claim that if you always completely finish something then:

(a) there is nothing left for other people to do and so they feel left out.

(b) it does not allow me to use my divergent thinking abilities and be creative.

Things were progressing nicely, but slowly. I had a scaffold tower in the lounge to which my wife was strapped. She does not like working off ladders (very sensible), but found a six-by-four-foot scaffold tower, with stout wooden boards as the platform, ideal to work from as it was not too restrictive. It was important that I encouraged and supported her in every way because, as you will have perceived, she is the persistent one who makes sure that everything is completed. Without her we would never have finished.

At last I was beginning to get my share of the cement mixer, as I was now mixing faster than wife was using it. Also, I now had a second wheelbarrow. Since I always cleaned mine out thoroughly, I had suggested that they should be labelled 'His' and 'Hers'.

She replied, 'If you don't clean mine out then I won't do any cementing.'

There's no answer to that, is there, so I dutifully cleaned out both wheelbarrows each day. With my own supply of cement, but with a different mix and using chippings in it as well, I was now into concrete and started on the kitchen floor. I won't bore you with the details, but will tell you basically what I did. As the floor was fairly smooth and level I put a plastic membrane on it, with battens on either side of the kitchen wall and poured the concrete on, levelling it out with a piece of three-by-two. It's not ideal doing it on your own as you always end up with some unevenness, but I felt I could live with that. If I could not, then I could skim it. It all came together much more quickly than I had anticipated, and in under two days it was finished. Within another two days I was able to walk on it without the fear of leaving size twelve footprints. Yes, there were imperfections, but I felt that I could live with them, and certainly at that moment in time I had no plans to do any skimming.

There were just a few days before we were due to return to England. The summer holidays would be over then and we had had the house for more than a year. It just did not seem possible. The summer in France had been so enjoyable – barbecues on the patio, all sorts of wine tasting, our new-found bubbly which tasted like champagne but wasn't and which appeared to fool all our guests. It's rare to get a champagne taste for beer money! However, more about that later.

We had decided that during the summer we would not do any formal entertaining, even though we now had a proper table and chairs in the lounge as well as a carpet. With this, the cementing done and everything painted, it looked like a proper room. It was at its best with the log fire burning, but in the temperatures that we were experiencing that summer, it hardly seemed appropriate. In case you were wondering, I had won the battle of the fire. Yes, it was an open one with a large wrought-iron basket, sitting upon two dogs – it looked great! We made sure that we always had plenty of champagne (substitute), orange juice and of course good wine and any amount of snacks available at all times for anyone who called in – that included the postman, who sometimes had time to sit and chat and have a glass of something with us. Can you imagine that happening in England? It's lovely that nobody seems to have the pressures that we have in England, or if they do have them, they seem to have the ability to ignore them and hope that they go away. I must try it. I say 'appears' because I have a theory that we often create our own pressures when there is no need. One of my grannies used to twist a well-known phrase and say, 'Always put off until tomorrow what you should do today or possibly put it off until the day after.' She died contented at ninety-five so perhaps she was right!

We had a good assortment of both French and English visitors, both separately and together. It was all casual but very enjoyable. Everyone was very complimentary about what we had achieved – it's amazing the things you say after a couple of glasses of wine! They were amazed at what we had done without any outside help, but only one of these visitors actually offered us any physical help. Having said that, we did have lots of offers to water the garden. The only problem was that apart from pots of geraniums, we didn't have that much to water. I wondered if they would be as keen to offer their services next year when the vegetable garden would be flourishing.

At last we almost felt that we lived in France. We felt that we had transferred our roots, and that they had taken. We were almost reluctant to return to England. However, return we must, not only for my younger daughter's education but also to work. We were planning to visit Hong Kong for Christmas to see my elder daughter so there was money to be earned to pay the fare!

It took more than a day to tidy up and pack and load the car. There was more to do than usual as on this occasion we were not returning to France for another six weeks. I was looking for ways and means, and reasonable excuses, which would allow me to return sooner, but I didn't think work commitments were going to allow it.

We made sure that we had a reasonable supply of wine. I can see you asking what a reasonable supply is? I shall just say that the allowance is now ninety litres each of table wine, or more if you can justify that it is for your own consumption, plus of course ten litres of spirits each. It makes the duty-free allowance on the boat look rather sick (anyway, duty-free is only VAT-free). We took less than our allowances, but I leave it to your vivid imagination to work out just how much less. The back of the car seemed extremely close to the road surface!

The journey from the house to Le Havre was now nearly half an hour quicker than it used to be. Let me explain, or you will begin to believe that I am either fantasising or have learned to fly! The new bridge, the one which we seemed to have been waiting for forever, was now open. Le Pont de Normandie, which crosses the Seine just outside Le Havre, reaches the other side just a couple of kilometres East of Honfleur. It is expensive, thirty-two francs each way, but you can get a season ticket which gives you twenty crossings for four hundred and twenty francs. We left at around 8.15 p.m. and were at the port just after 10 a.m. to be welcomed aboard by the crew of the *Pride of Portsmouth*, most of whom we now knew, for the journey back to civilisation (or is it?). Alas, we had no choice, but our time would come. Our conversation was full of what we had done, what we hadn't done and what we wanted to do – please note we said nothing about England! Even our daughter was getting enthusiastic and deciding that France was a lot more interesting than England. We each in turn said what we liked most about being in France.

My wife said, 'The peace and quiet, and lack of pressures.'

My daughter said, 'The clear skies at night, when you could see all the stars, and of course my trips to the hypermarkets for clothes shopping.'

I said simply, 'No television and no newspapers to read.'

One would hardly call us materialistic!

Chapter VIII

In some ways the time dragged, but yet in others it went by quite quickly. I was busy with work and really did not have that much time to think about France, apart from wondering what building materials I could get on the roof-rack – some waste pipe, some three-by-two and possibly a bundle of roof battens, but no plasterboard. There is nothing worse than wet plasterboard! One dare not risk it at that time of year. It is okay when my daughter is not in the car because then I can get four-by-threes in the car.

Surprise, surprise, the wine lasted and we even had a reserve to come back to – that couldn't be bad. I wished that we didn't have to lug cases of wine back, but until the Chancellor of the Exchequer got his act together and reduced the duty (somehow I doubt if he ever will as it is too good an earner!) then lug we would have to! Having said that, however, one *does* get a far better choice in France. This is particularly the case with me, if I can manage to get down to Bordeaux where the wine section in Carrefour is bigger than the average Tesco store. Did you think I was a Sainsbury's freak? I shop wherever I get the best buys and it could be any of the big multiples.

We were back in France for the half-term. We felt that we were back home as we crossed the Pont de Normandie. The cars had already reduced to a trickle – why can't British roads be like this – and by the time that we had passed through Livarot there was hardly any movement on the roads at all even though it was 8 a.m., albeit a Sunday morning. Where does hurrying get you. Nowhere – only to an early grave!

If I have one complaint about France, and it's only a small one, it's the fact that the hypermarkets do not open on Sundays. It's not that I want seven-day shopping all the time, it's just that we normally arrive in France on a Sunday morning and I would very much like to be able to stock up on cheese, pâté and fresh vegetables and of course the odd bottle of wine, although on this occasion we had brought a couple of bottles of wine with us – talk about carrying coals to Newcastle! Fortunately, on the route to Le Manoir there is a mini market. I am sure that the French would be very insulted if they heard me say it was small. It's just small compared with a hypermarket, and although well stocked, lacks variety.

The shopping done, we were at the house by ten o'clock and the sun was shining. We felt so glad to be there. Our postbox was stuffed with adverts from all the supermarkets – Super U, Hyper U, Intermarché and Leclerc. They probably contained all sorts of offers long since gone. I was sure that once we were in France permanently we would find them most interesting and take them up on many of their offers, but that was still a long way off yet. Apart from that, there was no post – the electricity bill had already been paid at the end of June so we would not get another one until December. We had given our French address to lots of our friends in England, but as expected nobody bothered or found time to write – they couldn't possibly all be that busy!

Everything was just as we had left it. The geraniums had survived, and as far as we could tell there had not been a frost yet, unlike in the Midlands and the North of England, to say nothing of Scotland. But certainly this time we would have to take them, indoors before we left. Quite where we were going to put them, just how we were going to cut them back and whether or not we were going to repatriate them were decisions to be made the day before we came back.

We hadn't gone into the house yet. My wife was checking the *cypressus lawsornii* and complaining that they had not grown as well as she had hoped. This was the problem with being 'instant'! I have told her so many times that the worst year for growth is the first year, and the bigger the trees you plant, the slower the growth in the first year. Personally, I thought they had done very well, particularly as we had not been able to give them all the attention we would have liked. What *had* done very well was the grass. Thank goodness I still had my old sit-on mower – the reliable Westwood which I had now had for fourteen years. It would not be worth much second-hand, but it was worth its weight in gold to me. Half an hour with that and everything would look so much neater and tidier.

'Isn't it time we went into the house?' I said. I unlocked the padlock on the cellar door and in we went. The cellar was just as we had left it. It was full of useful bits and pieces, various building supplies and countless tools. However, this could become a room as soon as I had a dry storage place. The lounge looked good, particularly now that it had been painted. I opened the wooden shutters – these were two wooden pine doors that I had trimmed and my wife had stained. They looked as if they had been purpose-built. To allow more light in, I opened the shutter door that covered the grilled window. It was actually like a room.

How was my kitchen looking? It seemed to be a bit dark with the window in the middle. It really needed something bigger and a door leading out to the garden as well. That would have to wait until the new year as this time my target was to plasterboard the walls and then set about assembling some of the kitchen units that we had brought over in the trailer on a previous trip. They were Rialto from B&Q, to my mind their best-value kitchen units, around one third of the cost of anything similar in France. It would be nice to get some of this done before we returned.

At this stage I did not know just what size or thickness the plasterboard came in – I was yet to start bringing it over from England. I had hoped that I might be able to purchase four-foot by three-foot, or if not then six-foot by three-foot (the metric equivalent of course!), but I did not want eight-foot by four-foot boards as they are difficult to move, transport, lift and fix – particularly on ceilings, although we would not be doing any of the latter. I would have to wait until tomorrow to find out. The floor was looking quite good, as far as concrete floors go, that is, but the laying of the tiles might not prove to be as easy as I had hoped. That did not really matter at this stage, however, as it was going to have to wait until the plasterboarding had been completed and the units assembled and put into position.

I was very fortunate that our builders' merchant was only two miles from the house. They were always very helpful and, interestingly, their prices were a lot more competitive than they had been last year. My only complaint was that they had a delivery charge, and this was regardless of the quantity that you have. In fact, the bigger the quantity was, the bigger the charge!

When I got there they *did* stock plasterboard but only in eight-by four-foot sheets. It was also heavier than the one I used in England. Ah well, it would be okay for the walls but not for ceilings, unless we had one of those fiendish machines that do it all for you. You place the board on top, wind the platform up and then wheel into the exact position that you want. You then wind it up further and so clamp it into position for nailing. It would be cheaper all round to get some four-foot by three-foot boards when I was next in England.

I reckoned that I would need sixteen sheets and then, seeing the thickness, realised that the battens that I had brought out with me were not really stout enough to take the weight. I would need some more. Once the plasterboard was loaded into the trailer and the battens on the roof-rack, I was fully equipped with enough material to keep me out of mischief, at least for a couple of days!

Have you ever tried carrying a sheet of eight-by-four plasterboard singled-handed? If you haven't, take my advice – don't! It is almost impossible, unless you have extremely long arms or have the physique of an orang-utan. In addition to this, the air must be totally still, as otherwise you will take off or collide with everything within four feet of you. Having struggled this way once or twice in the past, and ending up with two uneven pieces, which in turn had had very ragged edges, I was not even going to attempt it. This is where muscular wives come into their own. No, she is not built like an Amazon, and nor does she come from South America – just South Devon – but she does have an Amazon's strength and most definitely their determination! My wife must have heard me coming as she was on hand and delicately, if one can be delicate with something of this size, and without too much huffing and puffing, it was all neatly placed in the lounge. Perhaps, after all, wisdom *does* come with age, well a little bit anyway! To do this without any problems was quite an achievement really. Now that the front door was blocked off, one had to run the obstacle course. One had to go over the patio walls (no steps built as yet – not my department!), over the cellar step and into the cellar – quite tricky as there was less than six foot of clearance – weaving one's way between various piles of building materials and tools that we had placed, as it now appeared, somewhat haphazardly, up the earth slope-cum-tunnel and into the lounge.

That achieved, it was now batten time, and for the time being I needed no help or assistance, other than that supplied by my faithful hammer drill. A powerful hammer drill is an absolute necessity for this sort of task – ordinary DIY ones just won't do the job. You need a high-powered Bosch or something similar, plus of course raw plugs, screws, a claw hammer and finally a tape measure with a minimum length of five metres.

As luck would have it, the floor to ceiling height in this new kitchen was eight feet three inches, and as the room size was twenty feet by ten feet there was to be virtually no cutting or trimming and no waste. It's very rarely that you get a situation like this! I won't bore you with the details – there aren't many, really, and neither were there any incidents, apart from occasional swearing when my fingers or thumb got in the way. Well before midnight, having consumed a very nice bottle of Côte de Blaye, it was finished. My enthusiastic wife wanted me to start assembling the kitchen units immediately and no doubt would have been happy for me to work through the night so that she could have breakfast in there, despite the fact that there were no water or waste pipes in position – not that that would have made any difference as we were yet to be on mains water. That was something that came very much later!

Sitting down one evening, a very rare event for us and something that we almost felt guilty about, we realised that apart from some visitors calling and doing some shopping, we had not been out anywhere. We should really have had a bit of a mini-holiday. We decided to visit Dinan (not Dinard), which is quite close to St-Malo but a little inland. It's a lovely old town with steep cobbled streets that lead down to the river. It's where all the craftsmen now work – blowing glass, carving wood, making pots etc. I suppose it is a tourist's dream – chaos in the holiday season but very pleasant in the autumn. The only disappointment of the visit was that we could not find anywhere to eat. It was not that all the restaurants were closed, although most of them were pretty empty, it was just that we could not find a menu that appealed to us! Fortunately we knew that on the way home we could call in at Le Cygne at St

Hilaire where not only would we get good food but a warm welcome as well. Our genial host would pretend he was not able to speak a word of English when in reality he was beyond A-level standard. As we walked in I noticed that the room was full of cigar smoke, together with the very familiar Gauloise. I said to our host that I thought that smoking was banned from all restaurants. He sighed and said, 'Yes, but it is a bad law' and just shrugged his shoulders. Can you see anyone doing that in England?

We started our meal with a rather nice coarse duck pâté, followed by John Dory cooked in a mustard sauce. To finish, there was a raspberry coulis. This was all perfectly presented, as only the French know how, with the service to match. We bemoaned the fact that it was forty miles from the house, although that might have been a good thing as otherwise we would have been there most weeks and would got absolutely nothing done! Not that much got done for the rest of the day, anyway. But I am pleased to say that our feelings of guilt had disappeared.

I don't know whether I should really be admitting this, but nearly three years after we bought the property we still did not have our own mains water. There was mains water available to the adjacent barn and so cursing at the same time we had to transport countless large containers of water to the house. This was not really for washing and not for drinking, because you only drink wine in France, but so that we could water in my beloved *cupressus leylandii* – all one hundred and twenty of them! No, we weren't planting a forest – just wifey's idea of an instant fence! In hindsight I am not complaining as they have already exceeded three feet in height, but at the time it was different.

When we bought the house the details indicated that there was a mains water supply. What it should have said was that mains water was available! No problem, I thought. When we were ready I would just call and see the local *Maire* (the local power controller throughout France)and we would be connected in next to no time. If only that had been true. This time, at least, it was not all my fault!

I knew where the mains water entered the site and just where our connection could be made, and so to ensure that everything was ready and there would be no hitches I hired a mini-digger plus operator to dig out a trench a metre deep. This he did, with frequent loo stops. Every time my wife came out to see how he was progressing she found him standing by the hedge relieving himself. She gave up! He dug the trench up to the tarmac and then the other side, but refused point blank to dig through the tarmac. For that, he said, you must have the permission of the *Maire*. I tried to get him to call the *Maire*, but with no success. I thought that if he did it we might short-circuit the system.

After two hours of work we had been nearly there, but now we had to abandon things – total frustration! I decided that I would go to the farmer before proceeding any further. Although the stretch of road/track under which the water supply had to pass was tarmacked, I did not think that it was a part of the highway. If it was not, then surely it must be out of the *Maire*'s jurisdiction. The end of the week came and the farmer duly arrived. He just laughed when I asked him about the tarmac. It was his and the *Maire* did not have to give his permission, but what he did not tell me was that I still had to ask the *Maire* before I could get the water installed! Why do people always imagine that you understand totally how their system works – could it possibly be because my French is that good? How I flatter myself! It was the postman who solved my problems. On this particular day he had time to spare and sat down with us for an aperitif – may I add that he only drank orange juice!

'*Le maire* is *le grand contrôleur*,' he said. 'If you do not get his permission, *les gendarmes* will call.'

That was not very reassuring. I didn't fancy getting locked up for disobeying a law that I knew nothing about, but I suspected that, just as in England, 'Ignorance is no excuse and will not be accepted!' As a result of all this, I, very obediently, went trotting off to see the local *maire*. After a fifteen-minute wait I duly entered his office. He was pleasant and helpful, totally different than what I had been led to believe. How urgent was this water connection, he wanted to know.

He breathed a sigh of relief when I said, 'Not terribly.'

Since we had waited more than a year already, what was a couple more weeks? He told me that the man who did the water connections was ill in bed and liable to be there for another two weeks at least, and there was also a waiting list! However, he did give me a form to take away, fill in and return to him. He would let me know just when the work would be done!

That left me with a problem, something that I did not want. Should I dig up the tarmac myself and place boards over it so that the tractors could pass, or just not bother? The whole thing might be open for ages, and the boards could break. But the workmen could turn up and, finding nothing done, go away again, and I would be back at square one! I would clearly have to think before returning the form. My wife was not going to be too pleased. She imagined that once I had spoken with the *maire* there would be a cascade of water and a shower would be available on demand!

Surprise, surpass, my wife did not take the news too badly. She even found it rather amusing that the workman was ill in bed and he was the only one who could do it. We decided that the whole thing could wait, not only until the workman had recovered but until he had cleared his backlog as well. As it turned out we waited an awful lot longer than that because my wife was definitely not keen on me digging up the tarmac, either with a pneumatic drill or with a mini-digger. She has faith in my simple DIY abilities, but not when I suggest them. In her eyes, using big machinery is for the professionals only. She could be right! Anyway, the time went by and the worker was still ill, so thoughts of installing the water became less important. After all, we had managed this long without it, and no plants had died (including my wife's forest). We had also still managed to remain reasonably clean – at least I think we were. Nobody stood that far away from us when they talked to us, or at least not that I am aware! I always reckon too much water will weaken you anyway, particularly if you drink too much of it.

So on we continued, until the day that our lovely neighbour, Aimée, decided that enough was enough and that something should be done. She decided that it was not right that we did not have our own water supply. She reckoned that I had gone to the wrong *maire* anyway – the problem of living on the boundary. Both *maires* can claim jurisdiction, should they so desire, and they do, as any service coming in gives them local tax – a continuous tax dependent upon consumption! May I add at this stage, in my defence, that I had visited the local *maire* in one direction a year ago and made an enquiry about a water supply. You have to do this because (a) the local *maire* likes to know everything that is going on, (b) any service coming in is liable to continuous local tax, i.e. the more you use the more local tax you pay, and (c) if you want to dig up the road you have get the *maire*'s permission. As you can guess, the summer came and the summer went and the water position was stagnant – it was a good job we weren't drinking it! One Tuesday afternoon we had the summons from Aimée. We were to meet the other *maire*, with Aimée and also our French-speaking Aus lady, just in case we had any translation problems, and everything would be sorted out immediately!

The *maire*'s office was on the first floor of what had been the old school. To say it was in disrepair would perhaps be being polite. The stairs just about supported one's weight, plaster was hanging off the wall and the wiring, new though it was, was somewhat exposed. Still, we had not come to admire or to comment on the architecture or the state of the building. We were here, we hoped, to do business. Aus was all dressed up, looking very smart, with high-heeled shoes on. Perhaps she thought she had been invited to a wedding! Aimée was much as I would have expected a retired primary school teacher from Paris to be – plain, smart but practical. The resident *maire*, a seventy-year-old lady who was apparently a force to be reckoned with, was not there today. That was a relief. She had been replaced by a young female civil servant. This suited Aimée well as she was able to use her pleasant but direct approach without any fear of being thwarted or attacked in any way. She explained to the temporary *maire* that we had no water and that this was terrible.

'When would you like it connected,' the *maire* enquired.

'*Immédiatement*,' Aimée replied. 'You will, please phone the water company now.'

The French are always polite! The *maire*, a pleasant but unassuming lady was not used to being handled like this. She kept looking at Aus and me – I think she thought that we were married and that my wife had merely come along either as an interested party or for an afternoon's entertainment, but she did as she was told and telephoned the water company. Someone would come shortly and look at the situation, calling at Aimée's if we were not there. The Aus had not been required as a translator. We returned to Aimée's for tea. After about half an hour, Lucien and I were enjoying a glass of Calva – he is only allowed it (begrudgingly!) when I am there – when somebody came down the path dressed in an anorak.

'That would be funny if it was the man from the water board,' I said, and it was.

We left and he came to survey the scene back at Le Manoir. Aus was still in her glamorous outfit, ensuring that we understood everything that was going on. She needn't have worried because we did, but her presence was reassuring nonetheless. He surveyed the scene and within ten minutes he was off saying that he would be back tomorrow.

He was as good as his word. At eight o'clock the next morning, when fortunately I was up but my wife was still slumbering, he turned up with his team – a lorry towing a compressor-type thing and a digger. Can you imagine that type of service in England? If you can, tell me, as I might even think of having a pied-à-terre there! Now they'll dig up the tarmac, I thought. I waited and waited but nothing happened. The digger was busy and the workmen were in the trenches that I had already dug on either size of the tarmac. Ah well, all I could do was wait. At this time I became aware of the noise of the compressor and thought they must be getting ready to use the pneumatic drill. Curiosity killed the cat and satisfaction brought it back! So I had to go and have a look and saw, much to my surprise, that they were using a micro-bore and had been for the last hour. Within minutes they were pulling the pipe through, and in less than half an hour everything was completed. The water was connected, the trenches were filled in and they were gone. And to think we had waited nearly three years for this to happen. It's sickening when you think that the trees were now well established and no longer needed constant watering. Still, it made washing that much easier!

So if you are buying a house in France, try and make sure that it is on mains water already and if it is not, *do* ascertain how close the supply is. We were okay because it was a matter of metres, but if it is not, make sure you have a good well or be prepared to spend a lot of money to get the mains connected. The same goes for electricity, gas and the telephone. If you want isolation but also the services provided, it could prove to be very expensive. Still, there's always a wind generator, bottled gas and a mobile phone! It's funny that although you have the desire to escape there are still so many basic things that you need, unless you become entirely self-sufficient. We try but we never seem to make it, probably because of the demands made upon us by our children. Still, if you *were* totally self-sufficient, it would probably take all the fun out of life. You would be totally organised and all the excitement would have gone and everything would be predictable – how boring!

Chapter IX

You will be forgiven for imagining that all we ever do is work and that we are not really aware of what is going on around us and not talking to the locals, so perhaps I ought to tell you a little bit more.

You will remember the artisan – the one who helped me over the *cambrioleur*. Well, over the months he visited the barn complex down the road more frequently, not working on the barns but working the land. On most of these occasions he had his wife with him – at least we assumed it was his wife. We always knew when she was there because her voice carried as if she was singing an aria at Wembley Stadium. From a good four hundred yards we could hear every word she was saying, even when the wind was blowing in the wrong direction. Poor man! He's ever so nice – I don't know he can put up with it.

She is one of those friendly souls who likes to engage in conversation – a conversation of which the whole neighbourhood is totally aware. I became aware of this one afternoon last autumn when she was collecting cider apples from what had once been a large orchard. We used to have one too, but all that remains now are two rather tired trees, which I am not sure how to prune, and a magnificent cider press, complete with all the trimmings, including the sacking which was placed between each layer of apples and the wooden framing.

She called out, '*Aimez-vous le cidre?*'

That was a difficult one. If I said 'Yes' then she would either come up and visit me or expect me to go down there, but then I couldn't say no as that would be rude. It was a time for rapid thinking.

'Sometimes,' I replied, 'but I prefer Calva.'

I hoped to goodness that she did not have a still, illicit or otherwise, and wouldn't invite me down for that instead. Fortunately, she just laughed. She went her way and I went mine, and ever since

I regret to say I have avoided making conversation with her, although I do give her a cheery wave from time to time!

Talking of Calva, the question of whether it is illicit or not is an interesting one. Apparently the stilling of Calvados is one that is passed down, legally, through the female side of the family in Normandy and Brittany, and I believe that providing it's registered, it can be passed on to succeeding generations, although only one can do it at a time. Quite how much they can produce I am not sure, but judging from the stuff that I have tasted, unless you have a cast-iron throat then you are better off using it for cooking! To be on the safe side you are better sticking to one of the proprietary brands if Calva happens to be your tipple!

As I sit now I can hear the fair maiden's dulcet tones rending the air. The wind is not blowing in our direction so I cannot tell whom they are aimed at and whether they are endearing or abusive. I will be charitable and opt for the former – there is no chance of going a little nearer to find out. It is not the cider season, although the apples are forming well and swelling – the blossom escaped the sharp frosts that they had in England in April. The same goes for our grapevine which looks to be very heavily endowed with grapes, each only a little larger than a pinhead. With the amount of rain we have had in the past week I am anticipating a minimum of three hundred bunches. This is the second year of our winemaking. We plan to taste our first vintage on our thirtieth wedding anniversary, making the assumptions that (a) we don't run dry one night prior to that and get desperate and (b) that we are still talking to each other! Although the area is very rural, with no towns of any substance close by, and with few grand houses – I would not describe ours as grand, but noble, although it just might be grand *when* it is finished – it is surprising how many Parisians spend the summer down here, normally from April until early October. Hereby hangs a tale. Louis and Claire are from Paris and live in a large house immediately adjoining the local church – fine if you don't mind the clock with its positively enormous bells chiming throughout twenty-four hours of the day, including the quarters. We can hear it clearly from our house, which is nearly three kilometres away, so just imagine what it is like living next door! On the first occasion that we visited them it caused me to jump a foot, no, on second thoughts at least half a metre, as it chimed the quarter. Fortunately I did not have to put up with it when it chimed midday. I don't think I could ever learn to live with something like that!

The house – a *manoir* rather than a mini-chateau – is set in a large, formal and well-kept garden. You never see the gardener but you are always aware of his presence as the fruit trees are always perfectly pruned, all the roses, and there are many of them, are dead-headed as soon as they die, some even prematurely, and the grass is perfect for bowls rather than *Boules*! There is a feeling of grandeur long before you enter the house. The age and the period of the house are difficult to estimate, but I would suggest it is two or three hundred years old. If I was in England I would probably say that it was Queen Anne, both front and back. I say this because so often in England you come across a Queen Anne front and a Mary Anne back – the front was to impress and the back did not matter! In France I would say Louis Fourteenth. From the outside it is clearly sound and in good repair. Within the house the rooms are all of regular shape with high ceilings. It is a long but not a wide house, the depth being the rooms plus the corridors and back staircase (or was it front?). The rooms are very plain, as so often they are in French houses of this period. I could see my wife just itching to get her hands on it with her design ideas – not to alter it but to bring back the magnificence that it surely once had! To me the most impressive part of the house is the staircase. It is stone with a wooden balustrade, striking without being too ornate. It in turn leads to what in my mind is the best part of the house – the attic. No, this is not a place for hoarding/storing the kind of items I have collected over more than forty years (who was rude enough to say 'junk'? You won't be sharing a bottle of Médoc with me!), but a magnificent space that stretches the length and breadth of the house. It is uninterrupted apart from various chimneys, with wonderful buttresses of oak – so wide, so thick and so long. It is architecturally magnificent and rather reminds me of the inside of a large wooden boat such as the *Mary Rose*, but turned upside down. It is indeed magnificent, but what can you do with it and how can you show it off? To replace these timbers, not that they need it, would in all probability cost more than the house itself is worth –

that is assuming that you can get beams of this size.

Anyway, back to Louis and Claire. Louis used to be the head waiter in a top Paris restaurant, and may still do some work there in the winter months for all I know. His English is very limited but Claire speaks good English. As is often the case, however, her written English is better. Each year we would visit them several times for afternoon tea, in particular on Bastille Day, which is also Louis's birthday. He used to get up (and dress up!) to all sorts of tricks which perhaps should not be described in any detail here (certainly not the stockings!) for fear of any embarrassment, but which were certainly enjoyed by all! For more details you will have to talk to him directly – preferably on Bastille Day! It was as a result of these visits, one particular Bastille Day, that Louis and Claire decided that because our house was so old they wanted us to have (on loan) a lovely Georgian mirror. It was nearly six feet in height. It was to be ours as long as we lived in the house but to be returned to him if we ever sold the house. It never quite worked out like that, probably due to my still-inadequate translation skills. My grammar is basically okay but I get my tenses wrong! We enjoyed having it, however, during the short time that it was at Le Manoir. It really was magnificent and we looked forward to collecting it and placing it on the wall. To show our appreciation I gave Louis a large earthenware cider pitcher and my wife gave Claire a Shopping Français bag that she had made.

The next day we duly arrived to pick up the mirror, which because of its ornate nature, had to be very carefully loaded into the car. Even with the seats down it was sticking out of the back. With blankets draped around it and over it and the boot tied securely, we felt happy about our short drive back home, even though it was over a very bumpy road. Carefully removing the blankets, with our daughter acting as foreman, we manoeuvred it out of the car and into the house. Even just standing against the wall it looked magnificent. It would look even better when it was in its permanent position. What we did not know, however, was that it was not going to be in its permanent position for very long. It had been a wonderful, hot summer... no, I'm not changing the subject, as this is all part of the story. Two days after the delivery of the mirror I was around the corner picking blackberries. As you would expect, the best of the crop were just out of reach. I came back for a pair of steps, not wanting to disturb anyone as it was siesta time. I climbed the steps and when I had nearly filled a large plastic bowl I slipped, or the steps did, and I landed in a crumpled heap on my rear end. I managed to get up but could hardly walk and slowly staggered towards the house. Just as I did, I heard a car approaching. Oh no, that was the last thing I needed! Who could it be? I certainly wasn't expecting anyone. Surprise, surpass, it was Louis, and there was someone in the car with him. It wasn't Claire – it was his gardener. Alas they had come to take the mirror back, he explained quite simply. His children had told him that he had had no right to give it away. I felt much more sorry for Louis than I did for myself – he was clearly very embarrassed. I am sure that he felt that he was fortunate that he did not speak or understand English. While we'd been talking I had almost forgotten about my very bruised backside – that is until I attempted to sit down. It was almost impossible, and it took me more than five minutes to sink, very gingerly, into a chair. When I told my wife about the mirror, she thought that I was joking. She didn't really believe me until she came into the lounge and saw that the mirror was gone. I was so gobsmacked that I forgot to tell her about my accident, until she saw the bowl of blackberries and thanked me for my efforts.

Three days after the incident as I was preparing for bed, my wife asked me, 'Have you washed since the blackberry incident?'

The cheek of it!

'Why do you ask,' I said.

'You are still very stained on one side with blackberry,' she replied.

No wonder I was still finding it difficult to sit down – that was the multiple bruising! The moral of the story is that if you can't pick blackberries whilst standing on the ground then don't pick them! Still, they *were* very nice blackberries and I am still enjoying them now, long into the winter. They bring back memories of childhood and going blackberry picking and there were always as many as you could want to pick. Nowadays the few that are available are very small and sprayed with goodness knows what, and you end up buying them at Sainsbury's at a price beyond that of strawberries! By the way I talk, you would think I have a thing against Sainsbury's! I can assure you that I haven't. I am just one of these dreadful people whom none of the supermarkets like. I shop totally according to price and have no customer loyalty whatsoever. I am here today and gone tomorrow, depending entirely upon price. Surely more and more customers must be working on this principle? Talking of supermarkets, it is interesting to compare their prices in England and France. In the early and mid-nineties it was most definitely cheaper to shop in England, which is probably why the number of holidaymakers visiting France dropped quite dramatically. This is not including the purchase of wine and cheese, of course. By 1997 the story was very different and overall I would say that you can live more cheaply in France than you can in England, which suits us now that we are. No doubt you have been taken in by the 'buy one, get the second one free' slogan, or the more cunning one, 'buy two get the third one free', and you still fall for it even though you are not even sure that you wanted one in the first place! There does not seem to be so much of this in France – just the strange (irresistible?) bargains that they have on wine – 'Buy 96 and get 48 free!' It sounds great, *but* the big drawback is that you cannot taste it, that is without buying one hundred and forty-four bottles! When we first went to Bordeaux, on our honeymoon in 1967, we were both very clean-living and knew absolutely nothing about the evils of drink, apart from Saturday-night drinking sprees at university after hard cross-country matches or rugby. It was difficult trying to do both, no, not the drinking, but trying to play competitive rugby and County/England cross-country matches most weeks in the winter, not to mention the athletics in the summer!

My old granny – it's amazing how many mentions she gets; it's a good job she is not on appearance money, although if she were still alive, I would happily pay her in kind – would have said that if you don't know what to drink then drink the same as the natives! Well, Bordeaux must have been one of the first places anywhere to have a hypermarket. It was enormous and quite an education as far as we were concerned. At that time where we lived in England, we used to shop in the little corner shop and wait, for what seemed to be an eternity, whilst the person in front of us had what seemed like an endless conversation about nothing! In the hypermarket there was wine shelf after wine shelf, which at the time meant little to me, but there were very few people buying. Yet there were lots of beret-wearing, red-faced men pushing trolleys full of bottles of red wine. Now just where were they getting them from? This is where the bowser came in. At the extreme end of the hypermarket these same red-faced men – there were few, if any, women, and those who were there, were not red-faced – were filling up bottles from what resembled a petrol bowser in the wall. At less than five francs a litre it seemed to be excellent value – it had to be with the quantities that the French were buying. Then came the sad realisation that I didn't have any empties to fill! Ah well, there was always next time, which I decided would have to be tomorrow or the day after at the absolute latest! In the meantime I would have to make do with a couple of bottles of Bordeaux – unnamed and non-vintage (and sadly in 75 cl bottles), at the princely sum of seven francs fifty a bottle, twice the price of the bowser wine!

I hoped that was not going to break the bank, although you may wonder when I tell you that the second part of our honeymoon (the first part was in a five-star hotel in Devon, just four days), which lasted nearly three weeks, was done on a total budget of less than two hundred pounds (we were in a tent by the way!). Whilst I am on that subject, I must share with you our first night in France after we were married. I can't think why, but we used the Newhaven–Dieppe crossing. It must have been some special offer. Anyway, we arrived at Dieppe late in the evening and the only campsite was full, but we were directed to what we thought was an overspill, which was a nice flat grassy area. It seemed perfect. However, when I went to put up my little two-man tent, normally done in two minutes, I found that I was on bedrock. And there was worse to come – but not until the morning!

Despite the cramped conditions, my wife insisted on putting on her frillies – it was nice to be in France! The worst came. At dawn we had a very rude awakening. We were camped on the training area for the French army. As I gingerly opened the tent there they were, marching up and down with rifles at the ready, clearly highly amused that they were disturbing the defenceless Brits. I decided that the best thing to do was to keep our heads down until they went away. This was not easy with all that racket going on, but eventually, after two hours, they did. The moral of this story is never camp in France on anything but a proper campsite! Even things there can go wrong, however, like the time we nearly ended up on a nudist beach, but that is another story. Why do things like this happen to us, sensible, forward-planning people?

Back to the cheap wine! Two days later we returned to the aforesaid supermarket armed with an assortment of plastic bottles to fill at the bowser. This felt very satisfying and I was very pleased with myself until we got to the checkout. There was no problem with anything until we came to the plastic bottles. The cashier, I noted, had charged me twenty-seven francs a bottle. I queried it and soon the supervisor was with us. What was I doing putting the draught wine into plastic bottles, he wanted to know. These were reserved for *six-étoile* bottles (yes, six stars!). How was I supposed to know that! However, I will never make the same mistake again. I apologised but that appeared to do nothing. She grabbed the two plastic bottles, said something incomprehensible (not that difficult with my level of French at that stage), and told the cashier to amend the bill. I almost felt a criminal as I paid the adjusted bill, but also very hurt. Still, at least I have the compensation that nothing has ever happened like that since, in nearly thirty years. Plus, when I checked my money I found that she had given me too much back – was this some form of compensation? You can't always get it right, can you!

Never leave a glass unguarded when Helen is around. If you do, you may well die of thirst! I will leave you with that one to think about. It's just that if there are ever two glasses on the table, then Madam's just *has* to be the one with the most in it, so whichever one you drink from you have lost – unless, that is, you drink from the one with the most in it as much as you dare and then take a great slurp out of the other one! I just do not think that I could be that mean, or could I?

My visits to the *boulangerie* were numerous, that is until my wife started making bread. She makes a very tasty malt loaf, but even with that, there is nothing to beat a nice warm crisp baguette. These innocent journeys often provided amusing incidents. The *boulangerie* had an excellent stock of wine, mainly Bordeaux, far better than the local mini-market. There never seemed to be more than ten bottles of any one wine, and then I realised why. The owner bought them by the case, took out two for his own consumption and then divided the cost of the case by ten and placed them on the shelves. Thus he had a variety of good wine, free!

One morning when I was in there I bought four, perhaps five, articles – yes, including a bottle of wine. While *la Grande Madame* began to add up the bill on a calculator, I asked why she didn't use the calculator in her head. She clutched her head and said, 'My head is full of wine and I cannot think, let alone add up!' So *she* was the drinker of the good wine and not her husband – how appearances are deceiving! Then, on another occasion, when I had not been in the shop for several weeks, I though she looked rather sad and asked her why. She said that her daughter had gone across *La Manche* to Bournemouth for three months to work. One minute she was laughing and the next minute she was crying. Being polite, I said that I knew Bournemouth and that it was only three-quarters of an hour from Portsmouth, where our boat docked. At that she rushed from the shop to the back room and came out clutching a piece of paper that she gave me to read. It was the address of the people with whom her daughter was staying. Did I know them and were they nice people? And would her daughter be safe there? Try talking yourself out of that situation, whilst trying to be reassuring at the same time! I said that although I knew Bournemouth, I did not know these particular people or the area in which they lived but I felt sure that they would be very nice and that her daughter would enjoy her three months there. I hoped to goodness that I would be proved right and beat a hasty retreat! You wouldn't think that one could get into as many scrapes as I do in such a small village! Perhaps I talk too much? Please don't answer that question as I think I already know the answer! Having said that, though, things like this never used to happen to me in England, and if they did it was only on very rare occasions. No doubt the lady from the *boulangerie* would tell me that it was the effect of the wine!

The only other local shop that I visited – come to think of it, there were not many others apart from the butcher, the florist, the radio shop and the cycle shop, and of course two or three bars, the latter compulsory regardless of the size of the town or village – was the Comod chain of mini-markets throughout France. It was always very busy and their stocks were more than adequate for one's needs. Also, the prices were quite competitive. Since I am someone who does not like waiting – is that the same as someone who is always in a hurry? Not quite, I think – my one frustration in the shop was that having chosen my fruit and vegetables, I would then have to have them weighed and the price written on the plastic bag. It always appeared, to me anyway, that whenever it was my turn the assistant-cum-cashier was always busy doing something else and I had to wait. Inevitable, I thought, until I realised that the only reason you had to have it done for you was because the French did not seem to be able to make the scales work properly. Relief, I thought until one of the assistants, realising my potential, started to get me to weigh other customers' green groceries! This was okay occasionally, but certainly not at every visit!

It was here that I was introduced to my lovely bubbly. Now, there is Mousseux and Mousseux. There are some that are little better than lemonade, possibly worse, and others that can be as good as champagne. I can hear the purists chortling disbelievingly. Okay, I will give you a blind tasting. However, as you would expect, you have to take care. In this particular area price does most definitely *not* indicate quality. In fact, some of the cheapest are the best, thus challenging the theory that you get what you pay for! There are lots of lonely, or apparently lonely, people in the village, who, apart from their shopping trip, probably do not speak to anyone else for the rest of the day. This was ideal for me and, I hope, for them as well.

There was one little red-faced, behatted Frenchman whom I used to meet in there on a regular basis. It was on the second occasion that I met him that he introduced me to his favourite tipple. He had done his customary shop – a little bit of pork, a couple of slices of liver, some Emmental and a baguette – and was now standing in front of the wine section. His selection was almost instantaneous. He patted a well-developed (by which I mean oversized and, in the past, over-indulged) stomach and picked up two bottles of the cheapest of the bubbly at less than eight francs a bottle. He said, '*Une pour mon déjeuner et une pour ce soir*,' and beamed at me. Somehow drinking that lot I did not think he would get much done during the afternoon nor be aware of it. With that he beamed at me and said, '*Bonne journée et bon appétit*,' and was gone. My immediate reaction was that if he could be that happy and healthy (well, relatively so) then eight francs could hardly be too big a gamble to take to find out if he was right. So I decided to join him and added two bottles to my already overfull basket.

Coming to the cashout I pulled out an assortment of small change, which was weighing down my pocket and which I had an urgent desire to get rid of. I passed over a number of single franc pieces. Alas they were not all francs. Two were ten-pence pieces which had got mixed in, something that very rarely happens as I separate my money as soon as we land. Anyway, at that time they were worth less than a franc, a mere eight pence. He was not prepared to accept them. I quickly found some more francs and then asked him how he had noticed them so quickly. He said that he had just got back from a holiday in England. Had he liked it, I asked. It was very busy and the roads were very crowded. Where had he been I wondered? To Cornwall, and out of season. It just shows you how uncluttered the roads are in much of the Mayenne.

How is the house going? Are you still working, and is it all complete? I hear you ask. The answer to that is 'okay', followed by a 'yes' and a 'no'. Sometimes one is all enthusiastic and one hardly stops to eat or drink whilst on other occasions you wonder if it is all worth the effort. Fortunately, these periods of doom and gloom are very brief, and when we do feel like that we get out the photographs of what it was like before we started – that's bound to cheer one up! If you think about it, considering that we have had no outside help whatsoever and the immensity of the task we are doing quite well. We still may make it by the Millennium and get it back to its pristine glory, although it's funny how one slows up once one has moved into the house. Does one sit around more or is there an air of complacency? I'm not quite sure.

There are times when things happen which cause one to work both efficiently and rapidly, like the evening that I nearly exploded! It was the night that I completely installed the kitchen door – the one into the garden, in a matter of hours! I knew just where it was going to be placed, where the existing window was, but it did need some planning and preliminary work. But like so many things in life, that night it just happened, and with no planning whatsoever. Somebody upset me, and there I was with a lump hammer attacking this poor defenceless wall. What had caused the normally very passive me to act like this? Well, one of the matrons at my daughter's school was getting, if she was not already, totally unreasonable, and I had had enough! I could not get through to the school on the telephone – yes, by now we had a telephone, most efficiently installed the day after I requested it – so somehow I had to get some of the frustration out of my system, hence the lump hammer. In hindsight it was one of the best thirty minutes of work that I have ever done! The window was removed and the rest of the opening neatly achieved down to ground level. What I only realised the next morning was that there must have been, some-time in the past, a doorway there, or at least a window to the ground, as there were no jagged edges. It just goes to prove that aggression and frustration, if properly harnessed, can bring about useful results. The door frame was in, the door that I had glazed months before was hung and my wife was applying a coat of primer. All this of course also meant that even if I had been justi-fied, I was not as hard on the house matron as I would otherwise have been, and a task that might not have been achieved for many months had been achieved overnight!

I shall have to make a list of other tasks that require a certain amount of physical force and/or aggression to ensure their com-pletion and then wait for something/someone to wind me up. It will have to be something that has happened across *La Manche*! Funnily enough, it always seems to be caused by things involving my children!

In the time that we have had the house, less than three years, we really have achieved a lot, but we continually need to be con-vinced, probably because we have undertaken such a big project. We are convinced that we are mad because not only have we gone through the barrier of talking to ourselves, but we are now answer-ing back and are carrying on quite detailed conversations! We have decided, after the severity of last winter, that the main house is too cold from November to March, unless you continuously burn whole oak trees, something I would never do because I am a conservationist, or hang a hammock or two just beneath the ten-foot ceiling in the lounge/grand dining room/reception hall – we just cannot decide what to call it. We have an adjacent building, which at various times has been lived in, but in all probability over the best part of a century cows have been its sole occupants, with straw three foot deep on the first floor. It is compact, sound and small – well relatively small in comparison with Le Manoir so perhaps that will become our winter quarters but to find out if that ever happens I'm afraid you will have to wait as that will be another story! On a final happy note, when I was collecting building materials, a young student whom I got to know over the summer, came rushing over to see me.

'I've got it, I've got it!' he shrieked. He had got his degree and could now get a proper job! I felt as pleased as he did – proof, if one needed any, that there are lots of nice people in the Mayenne who want to be friendly – and perhaps even more importantly, proof that we have really been accepted.

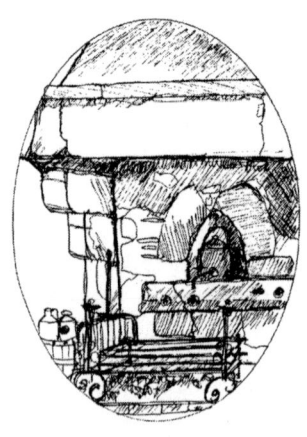

Chapter X

There were a number of plants that my wife was determined to grow. Nothing terribly exotic – some foxgloves and a rather nice daisy thing, well, it looked nice from the picture that she showed me, but alas she would always choose the wrong position for these potential specimens, at least that is what I thought. The foxglove was in very close proximity to the entrance of the barn where I was working – about six inches from it. I felt that it was doomed from the start but despite my protestations she was determined that that was where it was going to be planted and I knew that it was more than my life was worth to protest – I remember that somewhere from my O-level Shakespeare.

Initially it grew very well, and when it was about nine or so inches tall my wife said, 'There you are, I told you so. I told you it would do well and that was the right position.' I knew that was tempting fate but said nothing, and then within minutes of her saying that I had garrotted it with a six-by-four inch oak beam. I was speechless, having perpetrated the deed, but not so my wife. She screamed! I was spellbound. I didn't know what to say, and then suddenly she said, 'Get me a splint and some string!' Who was I at that stage to question her sanity? I did as I was told and duly brought two bamboo canes and some string. She muttered something under her breath, whether this was cursing me or just reassuring the plant I just don't know, and she very gently tied the plant up, even though the main stem had split down the middle. She added a bit of Sellotape and then watered it heavily. That night, and the next day, it drooped, and I was tempted either to pull it up or to deliver the last rites or both, but it was her plant so I left it. Miraculously, not only did it survive, but it has since flourished – she must have green fingers. The same thing happened to her daisy thing, when a cat or some other fiendish wild animal dug it up and left the plant almost rootless and certainly very dry. The same treatment led to a total recovery. I eventually plucked up the courage and asked her what the secret was. She said, 'You talk to them, be nice, as you should be to me!' I knew that I should never have asked!

As a result of all this, and many other things that she has cultivated, the garden is looking very nice. It has lots of colour, it's not too formal and it's something that will mature and expand over the years. I do do my bit – I do all the geranium cuttings and make sure that things do not get pot-bound, and of course carry on with my vegetable patch, amongst the weeds. I don't really enjoy weeding!

Yesterday I noticed some magnificent poppies in the garden. I hope to goodness that they aren't...?

Talking of gardening, a subject which has many words that one doesn't understand, not necessarily because of their Latin origin but just because they are long words, calls me to ask if you know what the word 'manifestation' means. I do in English, but clearly did not in French. I thought that I did until I saw it on an illuminated board on a tollroad. I realised that there must be a demonstration of some sort or another, but what on earth was being demonstrated? I was to find out very soon!

Travelling from Le Havre, having used the Pont de Normandie, we decided to use the tollroad to Caen for a change. It would not speed things up particularly as the journey was slightly longer, but we wanted to add a bit of variety to our journey. As we approached our exit, we noticed an illuminated sign above us on the tollroad saying 'manifestation', nothing more. Leaving the tollroad at Caen, and still seeing no manifestation, we reached a roundabout which was blocked with traffic. It seemed to be all lorries. Ah well, another traffic jam I thought, so I obediently, like a true Brit, joined the queue. Ten minutes went by and nothing happened, although I noticed a few cars going by on the left and assumed they were just turning left shortly. After a further five minutes I had had enough and gingerly pulled over to the left outside the lorries. I found that there was a clear passage to the roundabout about half a mile ahead. Reaching the roundabout, we saw that there were lorries everywhere, but there was just enough room on the inside for cars, not enough for anything else. We just managed to get through, and within minutes we were out of it. You have guessed it – it wasn't a jam but a lorry blockade, something at which the French are masters. If you see a sign saying 'manifestation', then you will know that there is a roadblock of some sort, and if you take my advice you will avoid it. I say this because the *gendarmes* and police are of no help whatsoever. They are in the same union as the lorry drivers. From then on, until we reached our destination, with the aid of our Michelin maps and my wife, who is forever becoming a better map reader (thank goodness!), we never touched another main road apart from crossing it. We were to find out later that most of the lorry blockades rarely interfered with the private motorist, but we did find some of their methods, such as setting bonfires in the middle of bridges and on roads, somewhat intimidating. Still, there are plenty of things to compensate for the Gallic overreactions, and at least by their actions they do seem to get things done, or at least cause things to happen here. Is there a message here, Brethren?

Chapter XI

Everyone who dreams of France, and those who visit for their summer holidays or even just for a long weekend, imagine balmy days, long hot summers eating al fresco and relaxing, enjoying the wine. Well, it can be like that but it can also rain stair-rods relentlessly, and in the winter it can get very cold and there can be quite a bit of snow. When it snows, even just a surface covering, my advice to anyone is not to drive in France. For some unknown reason the French drivers just do not know how to handle it. They drive very slowly down the middle of the road and when somebody comes towards them, they brake violently and swerve. Nine times out of ten they end up in a ditch, of which there are many on the minor roads in France.

I remember one particular morning in January, the year we bought the house. We were using the tollroad to Caen and turned down in the direction of Alençon. It was dull and cold but there was no sign of any snow, at least not yet. Some twenty kilometres later, after we had inconveniently turned off the main road, it began to snow very lightly – there was hardly a covering on the road at all.

'Should we turn back?' my wife enquired.

'No need whatsoever,' I said. 'We have less than fifty kilometres to do.'

She was not really convinced but decided, reluctantly, that perhaps there was no need. As we proceeded, just a few kilometres more, the chaos commenced! By now there was about an inch, at the most, of snow on the road, and driving conditions as far as I was concerned, presented no problems. But that was not the case for the French! In under a kilometre we came across half a dozen cars that had swerved off the road and lorries that had just stopped and whose drivers were talking, clearly with no intention of going any further. By this time my wife had turned a whiter shade of pale! I drove from one side of the road to the other, weaving in between and around all the stranded vehicles.

'Shouldn't we turn around?' she pleaded.

'There's nowhere to turn,' I replied, now even more determined to complete the last forty kilometres to the house. I honestly felt very sorry for my wife as she become even paler, but I reckoned that going back would be even worse. I am not as hard as I appear!

Within half an hour, and with little further ado, we arrived in La Ferté Macé. My wife looked positively dreadful, slumped in the front passenger seat, but my younger daughter seemed to have survived the ordeal without any ill effects! Fortunately I had a magic cure that I knew would revive her. It was not actually in the car but one that I could purchase as we passed Leclerc – thank goodness it wasn't a Sunday! I parked the car and dashed in just for this one item. The rest of the shopping could wait until later. I went past the clothes, the frozen food, the cheese and the vegetables. I was nearly there. I moved past the orange juice and bottled water, past the cider, past the wine and there it was – a bottle of Calvados! You may say, 'Calva at just past nine in the morning?' And so might I, but we were in a desperate situation and desperate measures were needed. One quick tot brought some colour into her cheeks, and after the second it was as if nothing had ever happened. I had just known it would work!

By this time the snow had got an awful lot worse and there were three or four inches lying on the road. In a way, however, this was good news as there was no traffic whatsoever, apart from the abandoned vehicles. As a result there were no problems with the remaining fifteen kilometres and we arrived relieved but relatively relaxed, hoping that the snow might get deeper and that we might well have an extended holiday. We *did* get an extra two days but I would have liked an extra two weeks. Alas, we no such luck!

The night after we arrived it snowed heavily, and I was pleased that we had a sound roof, pleased, that is, until I got up in the morning! Heavy snowfalls in this part of France are rare so we were surprised to find six inches of snow – not only outside but upstairs in the house as well! How could this have happened with an intact roof? Well, although the roof had recently been re-tiled, in France they never, or very rarely, put any felt on and they never seal it where the purlins touch the outside wall. There was a gap between every purlin, and this is where the fine snow had blown through – a full three-inch gap. We assuming for ventilation. Well, Not anymore! The gap is now both sealed and insulated!

It was one of those nights. Not only did it snow heavily, but there was a big drop in temperature and, come the morning, we had no water! In addition there had been a power cut. Fortunately that had not lasted long. But the Butagaz had frozen. It serves me right for using butane instead of propane – isn't hindsight a wonderful thing! I could have sorted out the gas if I had had some hot water, but I did not even have any water, let alone the means to heat it – a double chicken and egg situation! With that, the electric power came back on and I hurriedly filled a saucepan with snow and put it on the stove. It's amazing how little water you get from a saucepan of snow, but it was sufficient to thaw out the gas cylinder. There was only the water problem to sort out now. My wife was by now gathering buckets of snow so that at least she could have a cup of tea, whilst I was trying to remember just where the water pipe came into the barn and living in hope that it was only above this level that it was frozen, and not in the main itself. I eventually found it down a hole at least a metre deep, which had sensibly been stuffed with hay and straw. It was unfrozen at the main and the pipe was only frozen just where it came out of the ground. Whilst the problem was not solved, at least I knew where I should start. While my wife's back was turned I stole her water – the snow that she had collected and then melted – but she forgave me when within two minutes we had a water supply.

So you see you *can* get bad weather in France just as you can in England, but I am convinced that it never seems to last as long or to get one as stressed as it does in England. It's got to be because of the pace of life – a snail's pace!

However, do not be put off by this, because every year we have been here we have had absolutely scorching summers. The hot weather is not always continuous and there are intermittent thunderstorms, but there is a quality to the weather (assuming that you like the sun) that cannot be matched in England.

One problem that the hot sun *does* bring is the fact that we have nowhere to cool off. We can't go for a dip in the sea as our nearest beach is more than seventy miles away and it is not a particularly clean one. As you can probably guess, my wife is angling for a swimming pool.

'One day,' I said, 'when everything else is finished.'

She replied, 'If that's the case then I will push you in complete with your wheelchair and won't throw you a lifebelt.'

And I thought that charity begins at home! I suppose we will do it sooner rather than later, but I do not think this year!

As far as we know there are very few English living in our immediate area, apart from someone with a small retreat which he visits irregularly. But a few kilometres down the road we do have a lovely French-speaking Australian lady who spends half the year in France and so lives, in theory, in perpetual sunshine. She is so kind and so helpful that as a result she gets taken advantage of by all and sundry, but with guidance and tuition she is now able to say no without feeling guilty, well not too guilty. It is through her that we have met lots of interesting French people, and of course she was important with regard to the water connection! Whenever we are away she looks after the garden for us and in return we help her with things like her car – changing wheels, checking her oil, etc. When she came back from Australia last time she found burst water pipes, even though she was convinced that she had drained the whole system. Like virtually all houses in France, the house was plumbed in copper – not a medium that I like as I always manage to get the solder to go the wrong way, i.e. away from the joint rather than into it. For years I have only used plastic, for both hot and cold water systems. Fortunately for Aus, I had sufficient bits and pieces left over from my work so I was able to cut the burst bits out of the pipe and replace them with bits of plastic. Fortunately the copper fit tightly into the plastic joints. Six months later it is still working, but one wonders what will happen if, and when, we get another severe winter.

Chapter XII

I am sure that I have never come across such a profusion of birds as we have here in France. Most of them would be considered mundane by serious birdwatchers, unless they were doing a census, but it is nonetheless lovely for me to hear them singing from morn until night and even through the night. The lovely thing is that most of them are very tame. I guess this is because they return to the same territory each year, and in our case see about four people other than us.

My favourite is probably the chaffinch as he sings all day, perched high on the chimney stack above us, but I can't forget the contribution of the thrush, the greedy starlings, the blackbirds, the comings and goings of the house martins (or are they swallows?), the thieving magpie and the two little wrens who come for a drink every time I go into the barn and turn the tap on. Added to this is the owl, a barn owl who used to live in our attic and keep it rodent free. Alas we have had to ask it to find alternative accommodation as we work on the house. This it has done to our mutual satisfaction – it has moved to a nearby barn and we still hear it most evenings.

Then there is the big black bird, which at the moment is the only name that we have for it! There are a pair of them and they live very close to Le Manoir. As far as we can gather, they have always been here. The locals call them buzzards. All I can say is that they are damn great buzzards, more the size of an eagle judging from their wingspan and certainly bigger than a peregrine falcon, of which there are quite a number in the area. But why are there only two? Or is it that we see a different two each time, and in reality there are more? By day they do not seem to have a call (it could be that I have missed it) but by night they have a shrill, piercing call that is much higher than one would have expected from their size. The male is the larger and heavier of the two, something that you become very aware of as you drive down the road. It is so heavy that it has great difficulty in getting over the remaining hedges, not that they are that high. Either it isn't aware of a car driving at about five miles per hour behind it or it just doesn't care. 'Glide' is the wrong word to describe its passage. It moves the way a helicopter moves, just gently flapping the tips of the wings, the rest of the wing barely moving. The female is much more graceful. She does glide and has a much higher flight path. On what it feeds we aren't sure, but we have seen it dive-bombing crows and also carrying, what looked like a newborn lamb in its talons. There have even been times when it has circled above us as we lunched on the patio, giving us more than cursory glance as its wings cast a shadow over us. Needless to say, when that happened my wife beat a hasty retreat.

I would love to find out exactly what it is and why it inhabits such a restricted area. The locals say that they are here and nowhere else. But the thought of making this too public worries me, however, as I do not relish being invaded by a load of bird-watchers. I could tolerate one or two, perhaps even half a dozen. The trouble is we all know what happens (in England anyway!) if you find a rare or unusual species, or think you have. Within hours you are invaded by hundreds if not thousands of very keen ornithologists. I came to France, to the Mayenne in particular, to avoid such confrontations, for peace and quiet, so alas I must keep my location secret and so protect myself from the invading marauders! If they *did* arrive, my only escape would be through the tunnel and we still haven't discovered that yet! We are still sure, however, that it not only exists but also probably almost in its entirety!

Talking of the tunnel, my wife was convinced that she had found the entrance. To the side of the house – what I call the back-side, facing north – my wife found two iron pins, some two feet or so apart, on which clearly a gate had been hung. The ground also dipped away. Were there steps below leading to the tunnel? She was convinced there were, but I felt there would not be any. I thought that there might be a cellar, but not a tunnel. My reasoning for this was because the tunnel would have been built in medieval times either as a means of escape or to allow the monks (and others) to pass unseen from Le Manoir to the chateau – absolutely vital during the Hundred Years' war! It would therefore have been within the building rather than outside. However, it was still worth doing what I call a probing dig to see just what we could discover. It might just be a rubbish dump, but that in itself could be very revealing, as we had learned from other houses that we had lived in.

So far we have dug down just eighteen inches and have really found very little – only one complete bottle of around fifty to one hundred years old and two broken ones. Certainly this is a task for later on, when everything else is completed, or if we have guests staying who have nothing to do. My daughter suggests that we have a tunnel party, asking guests to bring two bottles (full) and a shovel (per person) – this sounds like an idea worth pursuing! We have a house rule, by the way, that if anyone comes uninvited and stands around for longer than ten minutes, they get given a job of work to do. No wonder we don't get many 'drop-in' visitors, and when they do come, the ones who know, stay a maximum of nine and a half minutes!

I still feel that the entrance to the tunnel lies within the house, not in a wall because of the structure, but in the floor, probably in the cellar. Because that is my muddly store and where the cement is mixed, however, there is little chance of any serious exploration taking place there, at least not for another year or more.

I have just realised that I have hardly mentioned our various neighbours, other than the ones that we see regularly. I have talked about the family from Paris and their wonderful hospitality which, sadly, because of the *affaire domestique*, was short-lived. Our nearest hamlet, one could hardly call it a village, is less than a kilometre away. It is more or less owned by one family, our farmer friend from whom we bought our house.

The farmer, who is also a professional musician (classical, I think), spends most of his time in Paris, coming down to tend his crops on an as-and-when basis. The house where he lives is very basic, although spotlessly clean. He does not have many worldly possessions, not even a television set, something that is most unusual for the French. His uncle lives next door and opposite are Aimée and Lucien and their two neighbours – two Frenchmen in their late thirties, or early forties, christened by my younger daughter as the 'Brothers Grimm'. They lease their land but I gather they are perpetually worried that when the lease comes up for renewal either they will not have an opportunity to renew it or the cost will have risen. Because of this they will not spend anything on upkeep or improvements, and as a result it has no running water, no electricity and just a privy at the end of the garden. This is unbelievable when all the services are available just metres from their land. They are both presentable and, we gather, would like to get married, or at least have some female companions, but as you can imagine when the young women visitors, who are rare, see the conditions in which they would have to live, they make themselves extremely scarce! This is a problem really without a solution – sad in this day and age!

We wondered just how many other houses in the surrounding areas were like this. Many, or probably most, of them seemed to have electricity, but still most of the houses had water pumps outside – were these for show or were they their only water supply? The only way to find out would be to knock on doors and ask, but I was neither sufficiently interested nor nosey enough to do that! What we could be certain of was that nobody took advantage of the services that they received in the way that they do in England!

Noticing how well the grapes are doing reminds me of the wine – not that I take much reminding! Even though we are some way from the actual wine-producing areas of France – it is about two hours to the nearest – we still get quite a good selection locally. If you want wine from a particular area, however, especially if it is not well known or is of limited production, then it is best to go to the area where it is produced, although often you end up paying more for it, particularly if you buy it from the grower direct! Over the years we have tried the lot, or most of it from the *vin ordinaire* (at fifty pence) a bottle to the Grand Cru (at twenty pounds plus). By and large in life you get what you pay for, but that is certainly not always the case with wine. It probably *is* true at the ends of my scale but not so in between. The fifty pence is drinkable but is better for cooking. Some of those in between, at little more than a pound, are quite superb and yet others are positively dreadful. Once the Beaujolais Nouveau is out of the way, I look forward to the following spring when the new wines will be on offer, not the ones for putting down but the ones that are fit (hopefully) for drinking at the time! Each year we find something new, exciting and enjoyable but our pleasure never lasts for very long. Oz Clarke and his mates start writing notes in *The Daily Telegraph* and before you know where you are the lovely wine that you personally discovered has been stripped from the shelves. Hindsight is a wonderful thing. I was once left wishing that I had bought a hundred cases instead of just two of a very drinkable Côte d'Or Sauvignon. I spent a miserable and dejected two weeks looking for a reasonable alternative and ended up disappointed.

We vowed that after this most recent experience (my wife agreed that I have a good palate!), in future years whilst she roamed the supermarket, I would bring a dozen different bottles of wine that appeared to be promising out to the car and taste them. There would be no waste – anything thought to be not suitable would be recorked and used for cooking. This way we would get an adequate supply – more than adequate you might say – of reasonable wine. I say this in case you are not aware that you can get four hundred bottles of wine into a Fiat Tipo, that is assuming your wife walks home! How many less if the wife refuses to walk home it depends on her weight and I have been totally banned from mentioning that topic! If you reckon that a full bottle of wine weighs something close to a kilo you can work it out yourself!

You would imagine that as a result of this bulk buying my cellar would grow, but alas it does not! I am too generous with my tastings, I say. My wife fails to pass comment, most unusual for her. Is she trying to tell me something?

I rather enjoy the more expensive Médocs, the Cru Bourgeois Médocs, the Paulliacs and the St Estèphes, but the selection in the north is not that good and the prices in the supermarkets increase the further north you travel. Just imagine if your bottle of wine from Sainsbury's in Inverness (assuming that they have a branch there!) cost a pound more than the identical bottle in Portsmouth – questions would be asked in the House! Consequently, we tend to wait until we go down south, apart from the occasional bottle that we allow ourselves to indulge in. Anyway, it always tends to taste nicer if you buy it in the region where it is from. The point that I made earlier about buying direct from the chateau still stands, however. It is most definitely more expensive if you buy a case from the chateau, probably by as much as twenty-five per cent, that is of course unless you are buying cases in multiples of one hundred.

You would imagine that with all this going on that we had abandoned our building works. Well, we hadn't! Above our main room was a very large open space. It went right up to the eaves but unfortunately had a double metal bar bolted on either side of the two main support beams, preventing them from moving outwards. What made it even worse was that this was positioned eighteen inches above floor level. What on earth was I going to do about this? If I took it down, as I felt I must, then possibly the whole roof would cave in. I was determined not to ask a building surveyor as I was sure he would convince me, at a cost, that it was only put there to support the structure or to prevent it from falling down. What intrigued me was the fact that it was not rigid and did not appear to be in a condition of tension. Where was it positioned exactly in relation to the room below. Some quick measurements indicated that it was immediately above one of the main beams, so clearly it was there in case either the wall gave way around the beam or the end of it became rotten. If I could protect this, then in theory I could remove the double iron bar. I phoned Pierre for guidance, or rather to share my thoughts, as I had already decided just what I was going to do.

'Take it down dear boy,' he said, 'then if the building falls down at least you will know that was the wrong decision.'

I could tell that it was the wrong time of the evening to be talking to him!

Where the two beams went into the wall, on the front-door side there was clearly some rot. They were supported by two thick pieces of oak. I very much wanted to removed them, but discretion is the better part of valour and I didn't exactly want a pile of stone around me. What I would have to do, I thought, was to enclose them both in concrete pillars and then face them so that that they looked like a part of the original structure. How wrong I was! The two pillars took me the best part of a week to build, and whilst I was now totally happy with the downstairs and the fact that we would not have problems with either the beams or the outside wall, I did not know whether or not it was safe to remove my iron bars. There seemed to be several inches of sideways movement. They couldn't really be doing that much, I tried to convince myself. It was decision time. If I left them, then I could not see just how I could turn this space into a room or rooms. They would just have to go. Very gingerly and very slowly, not that speed was going to make the slightest bit of difference, I undid the bolts and released the rod on one side. Nothing happened. Then suddenly I heard monks chanting. Was this a message telling me that the building was about to collapse and to leave things as they were. It was very eerie. Then my wife shouted upstairs that she had put a plainsong CD on as she felt it was appropriate. I breathed a sigh of relief! Now came the big test, releasing the rod on the other side. It was now or never. I told my wife to evacuate the building just to be on the safe side. I crossed my fingers – only those on my left hand, as I was using my right. Four turns with the spanner and the bolt was released and the bar lowered to the floor. To my relief nothing happened and eighteen months on it is still as it was on that day. We're hoping therefore that nothing dreadful will happen now!

Now we had a wide open space of some four hundred plus square feet, with just one window and one of the three magnificent fireplaces. There was a staircase in one corner where you came in and another short flight of stairs – one would hardly call it a staircase as it was made from rough oak and had no rails – leading up to the attic. Just what were we going to do with it? For once we had no disagreements and did not even really discuss it. My wife and I both had the same idea. It would be two bedrooms and a snug-cum-library, the latter incorporating the fireplace. That was the easy bit. Even getting the sizes of the rooms worked out was simple. What was going to cause me problems was the ceiling height. I just felt that I would have to lower it to about seven feet six inches or eight feet. But how? Ideally, what I needed was a beam going across the length of the room but (a) I didn't have one, and nor did I know where to get one, and (b) there was no way that my wife and I could manoeuvre anything that size into the house and up the stairs, let alone lift it. Several days, and several good bottles of wine, later, I still had not come up with a solution but then I came up with a compromise. The roof sloped, so if I made one room quite narrow, say about seven feet six inches wide, then my verticals would not be that tall and could put my large beam across the remainder. At this stage I remembered that I had salvaged a rather large beam from the collapsed lean-to. I never throw anything away and I certainly don't cut up large beams for firewood, even if I am cold! On examination it turned out to be ideal. It was six by six and the best part of twenty feet long, although the last two or three feet of it were a bit moth-eaten! As anticipated, I could not lift it single-handedly. Just how we were going to get it into the house and up the stairs I did not know, but I reckoned it was feasible as long as the Amazon lady helped Tarzan! When I showed her the size of the problem she said, 'You've got to be joking,' so I knew at that stage to forget it for the moment. I would bring it up in a casual way later when perhaps I had worked out a way of lifting it, using mechanical aids, would make it less physical a task.

Our nearest town, and a small town at that, is Javron Les Chapelles, somewhere you would probably never visit. It is on the main road from Alençon to Rouen. It is clean and pleasant and has an excellent restaurant, which has been written up in *The Daily Telegraph*. It also has a very old church, which was built or rather commenced in 1046. The rest of the town is nowhere near as old, and it is hard to find buildings more than three hundred years old. Were the earlier ones replaced or was there never much here and it simply served the various farming communities around? Our house, apparently, has strong ties with the church and was supposedly built somewhere around the same time, but we have done no research into that yet. One thing that we do know is that the statue on the left-hand side of the fireplace upstairs, which is missing, was given to the church. They probably did not want the one on the right as it is minus its head. It's hard to establish just who this statue represents. Is it male or female? I plumped for it being a madonna but my wife is not so sure. However, we should be careful because there is a statue in the square outside the church of someone in armour. At first you may think it is male, but closer examination proves it to be Joan of Arc, who has close connections with this area. Without the head on our statue perhaps we may never know.

I don't suppose the town numbers much more than six hundred people, but they are all very friendly, passing the time of day and smiling in a way that nobody in England does. Certainly one gets accepted much more easily in France. People don't look at you and analyse you – they just accept you for what you are. My wife keeps saying that she doesn't know why we didn't come and live here thirty years ago. I wonder what would have happened, and just how our life would have been. Looking back there are parts of one's life that one would change, but certainly not all of it!

Well, we are well into the book, supposedly all about Mayenne, and I haven't mentioned the principal town – that is, Mayenne itself. I don't know the best way of describing it. If it were in England then I think I would describe it as a picturesque country town, on both sides of a pretty river situated in a valley. On one side is the old town and on the other the new. If you were driving from Alençon to Rouen then you would see nothing of interest, unless you class schools, hospitals, a small industrial estate and a hypermarket as interesting. Soon you would be out in the country again, not realising just how old Mayenne is and just what you had missed!

So where should we start? As you come in from the Alençon direction turn right at the first set of traffic lights. Within less than half a kilometre you are in a different world, particularly if the sun is shining. The river is straddled by an old bridge, which is less than forty metres wide but impressive nonetheless, and the water glistens in the sunlight. The old church with its many buttresses stands impressively on the skyline with the old castle adjoining it. I could easily stand on the bridge all day long and breathe in the ambience, apart from the fact that there were no pavement cafés around. These are all in the old town, past the church and behind the castle. It makes me wonder sometimes why I ever bother to visit England.

In this old part of the town there are, as well as the pavement cafés, all sorts of interesting shops, selling designer clothes and china. There is also the Monday market where, if you are walking on the pavement, you are quite likely to be approached by a farmer's wife with her basket of eggs, asking if you would like to buy some really fresh eggs. There will be eggs that she has taken from under the chicken that very morning. This lady I believe, and when I lightly boil the eggs when I get home I just know that she is telling the truth! I won't say that the market is particularly cheap, but at least you can see that you are buying fresh produce. In all probability most of it is also organically grown, primarily because most of these growers are doing things in a very small way and cannot afford the price of fertilisers. It is much more fun than shopping in a hypermarket, particularly if you hang around and wait for the end of the market, which is normally between twelve and one o'clock, depending on how business has gone. Then you can make an offer that they can't really refuse. I don't often do this, but it is quite fun occasionally. The French love it too!

Also in this area, alongside the river where it ends in a cul-de-sac is the Land of Noz. Actually it is just Noz. It is a mini-end-of-line warehouse, which sells anything and everything at knock-down prices. It's amazing how many Brits find it – it's got to be by word of mouth. The problem with Noz is that you never know when it is going to be good or bad. Sometimes (but not often) you feel like buying up the whole warehouse, sitting on it and selling it bit by bit but there are other occasions when you wonder just why you have gone there. Warehouses are probably best for car bits, toiletries and wine, although you have to be a bit wary of the latter as any wine more than three years old is liable to be something that a vineyard or supermarket has decided is well past its sell-by date and probably best if sold for wine vinegar. But there are exceptions to this. Here you have to do, as I do or rather did, in Bordeaux – go out to the car with half a dozen bottles and sample them. This is particularly important with Noz as anything good goes within a matter of hours, if not minutes – I wonder how they know as I have never seen other people sampling in the way that I do or are they just (lucky) gamblers?

Close to Noz, but not worth a visit in my book, although my wife does not agree as she likes poking through other people's cast-offs, is a so-called antique shop. It is more of a second-hand shop, as far as I am concerned where items, seldom more than twenty-five or thirty years old, are sold for about three times the price that they are worth. What is amazing is that they seem to do quite good and continuous business. Any budding Albert Steptoe could do a roaring trade there, particularly if father was in the tin bath eating pickled onions.

In addition to all this, they have open-air concerts in the square and one can take all sorts of trips on the river. There is much more to do here than you could ever imagine and once you have parked your car, and really it's not that difficult (it's also *free*), then everything is within walking distance. Every time we go there we see something new that we weren't aware of on the previous visit. Why do we go there so frequently, you may well ask. Well, it's because it is where we pay our telephone bill (every two months in France) and because, as I have mentioned already, we do not wish to miss out on any bargains in Noz. You can bet your bottom dollar that if we did not visit it one time then that would be the time when all the bargains were there.

At the bottom of the hill, immediately after you have crossed the bridge, there is a hotel. It is listed in the *Actueil*, which means that their cooking, etc. is up to a high standard. We ate there once. It was *nouvelle cuisine* and very pleasant, and not something that one would be disappointed in paying forty pounds for (for three, including wine). But if you ever you win my confidence I can find you at least half a dozen better, not that I am going to go around telling everyone because I am sure that my hosts, once they became popular, would quickly put their prices up! The thing I like about French restaurants, and that's virtually all of them, is that at lunchtime the table is yours for as long as you care to spend at it. There is no high-pressure selling and the service is the same whether you partake of a sixty-six-francs menu or a two hundred franc gourmet meal, with appropriate wine. And whilst a tip is appreciated, it is not necessarily expected. This is not the same in Paris, where not only do you pay inflated prices but a fifteen per cent service charge is either the norm or is expected! Everyone is so polite and makes you feel wanted, or have I been just lucky where I have wined and dined? I have only tried one of the street cafés, just for *un grand café noir* and a *tarte aux pommes*, together with a large cigar, pure peace and tranquillity! My wife reckoned that she would have to prise me out of my seat if she was ever to get me writing again. I keep telling her that these are the experiences that give me inspiration, but she is seldom convinced. If you think that she is a hard taskmaster, then you could be right! I do not need to be careful as I write this as she no longer hangs on each word I write – I think that died a natural death after I had written page fifteen! But she is still very grateful that I do not perpetually talk. In fact, there are even times now when she complains that I do not talk enough. Impossible to get it right, isn't it!

There is an awful lot that I could say about Mayenne, the town, but I don't want to spoil it for you. I want you to breathe in, explore it and find, as we did, a very interesting small town. It is seldom visited but it is one with a lot of interest where one can learn so much about central France and the people who inhabit it. You do not have to visit large towns with all the tourist attractions to enjoy yourself. It's also good that you have to use your non-existent, pidgin or fluent French to get yourself understood – the French in Mayenne are particularly good at pretending that they do not understand what you are saying if you persist in saying things in English. Fortunately, most of the Brits that I have met, no matter how unconfident they feel, are at least prepared to have a go – the Mayenees (my name for them) really appreciate this! I know that I am probably biased, but nowhere in France, that I have visited, as yet, is the general population as friendly or as willing to help as they are in Mayenne.

I remember the day, one lunchtime, when I was returning from the *boulangerie*. I came across a low loader onto our road (lane) and I had to go over on the verge to get by. As I passed, the car died on me. No sooner had I stopped than the driver of the low loader, who at this time was operating a digger, was at my side asking what the problem was. I did not have a clue, apart from the fact that my beloved Fiat would neither start nor move. Within seconds, or even a second, he had tried the ignition and was telling me that it was the starter! Barely seconds later, toolbox in hand, he was underneath the car. The disconnected wires were reconnected and the car was restarted. As much as I admire the AA, the RAC and Europe Assistance, nobody could have come to my aid in a more helpful and rapid way. And then he said it was nothing! Within minutes I was on my way and enjoying my baguette, neatly split and filled with Emmental, tomato and lettuce, sheer bliss, and a glass of Normandie cider. I might well have preferred a glass of Calva, but I doubt if much work would have got done if I had succumbed to that! One of the problems with France is that you have too many choices, and if you make the wrong one then you never achieve what you set out to achieve. Still, it's a good excuse and you can always say, 'Well, I would have done it but for etc.' I am convinced by that, but I doubt very much if my wife would have been! A Frenchman once told me to put off until tomorrow what one can't do today or if it's a real problem put it off until the day after – this sounds like very sound advice to me, even if you do not achieve all that you would like to! The more I live here, the more I realise that it is my kind of life. I can't help thinking just how lucky I am to be living here – how many people can say that?

At last we are now living almost permanently in France, spending less than seventy-five days a year in England. This is because I have taken the plunge and taken early retirement. It's not that early really but welcome nonetheless. There's not so much toing and froing on the ferries, although we used to quite enjoy that. It certainly produced some good leg-pulls! I bumped into a friend in England whom I hadn't see for ages and he asked me where I was living. Keeping a straight face with great difficulty, I said, in an affluent way that we spent much of our time on a large boat with our own crew, with excellent food cooked by a superb chef, an excellent wine cellar and even parking for our car. I could see that he was very impressed!

'It sounds big and luxurious,' he said. 'How big?'

Now I had to reveal all.

'Thirty-two thousand tons,' I said. 'It's a Channel ferry!'

To give him his due, although he had been duped, he did see the funny side of it! I wanted to tell him about some of our amusing experiences on board – and there are plenty – but I could see that he had had enough. Instead I will relate one of them now. One winter evening, we just caught the boat by the skin of our teeth. We heard the captain saying, 'The last vehicle has now boarded (us?) and we can depart – I apologise for the delay.'

He made it sound as if it was our fault! The boat was the *Pride of Le Havre*. We were on H Deck, the lower car deck, which is mainly used for lorries and coaches, and so we went to use the lift.

It eventually arrived and there was Albert, the Belgian accommodations officer. We entered the lift, along with two French lorry drivers who were clowning around. The lift started and then abruptly stopped. Albert pressed all the buttons in turn but nothing happened. He looked very worried! He used his intercom but was clearly getting nowhere. And then out of the blue, it seemed, suddenly over the lift intercom came a voice: 'Albert, I am so glad I have found you. We have a problem, where are you? There is somebody stuck in the lift!'

We all creased ourselves as Albert said, 'It is I who am stuck – I am in the lift!'

After that we heard numerous mutterings, not clear enough to be understood, and then eventually the lift moved upwards and we were greeted at reception with much hilarity! The number of times that story has been recounted is amazing. Our daughter has a constant reminder as she bought a little teddy bear that she christened Al Bear!

The crew of the *Pride of Portsmouth*, the sister ship, know the story well, but reckon that nothing like that will ever happen to them. They may well be right but at least the *Pride of Le Havre* has four engines that work all the time. The *Pride of Portsmouth* had some problems when one of the engines was out of operation for two months (it can operate quite safely on two engines), and then one night a second one went down and we were marooned in Le Havre for several hours. I found it quite pleasant. It felt as if we were on a cruise, particularly as we didn't disembark until eight o'clock the next morning. May I add that we were back on three engines by the time that we left Le Havre, and that on the next trip and subsequent ones all four were fully operational.

I think that with only one exception we have enjoyed every single trip across the channel. That one exception was being caught in the tail-end of Hurricane Lily – not an experience that either my wife, daughter or I would wish to repeat! On this particular evening the wind was howling and the trees were moving quite violently as we approached Le Havre.

'It's not going to be a comfortable crossing,' my wife said, but we were not too worried as we had been in force eight and force nine gales before. Then as we came into the harbour we noticed that the sea was breaking over the harbour wall, something that we had never seen before. The boat was fairly crowded and because we had made a late booking we had ended up with a cabin directly overlooking the bow instead of having one amidships – very pleasant in good weather!

Once on board we waited for the announcement from the captain. This duly came, with the captain apologising for a slight delay in our departure. The weather on the way over had been somewhat inclement. He told us that we could expect force seven to force eight winds early on in the journey, but that the Met Office had told him that the winds were diminishing and that later on in the night they would be force four to force five. That was comforting; I bought a newspaper and we settled down to a nice glass of bubbly, always guaranteed to give one a good night's sleep. If we had known what was to follow I don't think we would have been so happy! It was choppy as we left the shelter of the harbour and there was more than a light swell. Both my wife and daughter had already donned their armbands. Less than an hour later the full force of the storm hit us. To say that we were buffeted would be a gross understatement. My wife pulled the curtains back (a big mistake) to find that the waves were braking over the cabin window from above although we were fifty feet above the water line! We did not know quite what was happening, whether or not the boat would turn back or just how long this was going to last, but from previous experience we knew this had to be well in excess of a force nine wind.

My wife sat up all night, clutching my daughter's hand, and I had one of the most uncomfortable nights that I had ever had. We were relieved more than pleased to dock at Portsmouth. The captain apologised for the appalling weather conditions, which had clearly been beyond his control. But he told us that the weather forecast that he had been given had been wrong, and that instead of the wind backing off it had increased to wind speeds of around one hundred and five knots. He had never known anything like it in the English Channel in thirty years of sailing. He told us that we had hit, or had been hit by, the end of Hurricane Lily. I felt grateful that we had been on the *Pride of Le Havre* and not on the smaller boats that sail out of Cherbourg. We gathered afterwards that their experiences that night has been a lot more horrendous than ours – waves had actually broken over entire boats! Our one consolation was that if we could survive that, we could survive anything, and the likelihood of hitting another hurricane in the next thirty years was pretty remote.

Relieved to get off the boat, we were then subjected to a routine check by HM Customs and Excise – that we could most definitely have done without! Why had we visited France?

'Because I like it,' I said.

How often did we visit France? All the time they thumbed through our passports, looking at the stamps of Hong Kong and Macau, but they finally let us go when they noticed that one of our contact people on the passport was my wife's cousin – a Euro MP. The amusing thing was that I did not even have my full allowance of wine and was certainly not carrying anything that I should not have been carrying.

When I, with all my like-minded countrymen, decided that joining the Common Market was a good thing, I was under the impression that border controls between member countries would go for good, as would the duty on both wine and tobacco. Clearly, in the case of the latter, the various Chancellors of the Exchequer have decided that it is far too good a little earner to be abandoned lightly. Even though they lose out on about a billion pounds a year through illicit imports through Dover, they still end up with a surplus of eight billion on the excise account – something that they are not going to abandon either easily or willingly. And if they do, then other taxes will have to be increased! Still, these higher mathematics calculations do not really concern me anymore as I smoke very little and all my wine is bought in France.

We have not had a single customs check since that one, when coming into England, but whenever the car is heavily laden on the way out, usually with building materials bought from a B&Q warehouse, we inevitably get stopped. We're asked, 'Did you load this car yourself, sir?'

The answer is always, 'Yes.'

'Did you leave it unattended at anytime since then?'

Again the answer always has to be, 'Yes.'

We have to leave it unattended when we're shopping or when

we pick up our younger daughter from boarding school in Brighton – no guesses as to where she goes to school! I am not going to advertise them anyway. I see it as a good investment as her elder sister, who also went there, is already earning more than twice the salary of her elder brother, and he's not exactly badly off!

Harvest time is always busy. Our farmer from Paris arrives for several days with his complete family of six children. Amongst them is a midwife and a Benedictine monk in a black habit who wears trainers! It's all go, but only for a matter of days as the farmer tends to have a single crop spread over many large fields. I am not very good at estimating the size of a field, other than its area. An average size would be four hundred metres by four hundred metres, possibly more. This year the crop was wheat. After a day and half of the combine harvester, all was complete, that is all the grain had been harvested. In true French tradition nothing is wasted. The straw is gathered in and made into round bales, no doubt for use by the cows in the winter. I always thought that once you did this you left the fields fallow. This is not the case here. This is where the intensive farming begins. The soil is turned over several times and huge sacks of fertiliser arrived. No doubt in a matter of weeks a new crop will be sown and the whole process will start all over again. I am sure that one day the soil will utter a sigh of protest and refuse to bear any crops! However you can't but admire their organisation. I wish in a way I could be a bit like that with my life, but it would take the fun out of things as everything would be totally predictable. Organised to a degree I am, but predictable? I have my doubts!

Talking of crops, my grapes seem to be swelling quite well and it would appear that we are going to have as heavy a crop as we did last year. And that is without having done anything to the vine whatsoever! I am working on the principle of leaving well enough alone and doing absolutely nothing until I have a crop failure, that is a crop failure caused by anything other than frost. No doubt the experts would tell me that I am doing it all wrong and should be pruning and using all sorts of vine-culture tricks – ah well!

With regard to the other crops in the garden, that is apart from the weeds, they are a bit of a disaster. My excuse is that I haven't given it enough time, and probably not enough water either. I have picked about half a pound of runner beans and four courgettes the size of large peas, and my first, and probably the only, tomato that can be eaten has ripened. We are not going to be very self-sufficient with that lot! Ah well, there is always next year, I tell myself. The problem is that there is always so much to do. At least the rest of the garden is looking good. The grass is neatly cut, the *cypress lasawni* is growing well and the geraniums are turning the patio into a blaze of colour – I suppose that is the most important bit really. Somehow I seem to be much better at taking geranium cuttings than growing vegetables – can you eat geranium leaves with your salad? I am not sure that I'll try until an expert tells me it is safe. We have an expert in the family, actually. My older sister is a plant pathologist but I won't ask her as I doubt I would get a straight answer. She would just say something like 'Most plants are edible if they are treated and prepared in the right way', which would tell me absolutely nothing! One thing that I *would* like to sample, but I suppose I am frightened to, is one of the exotic mushrooms that I see growing around the neighbourhood. They are very large in size and very brightly coloured. I do notice that they are very rarely there for long, so someone must be cooking and eating them. To the best of my knowledge nobody has 'passed on' in the area lately. What I need is courage, I tell myself. 'What you need is expert advice,' my wife says, 'and that is not something that you can pick up from a book.' She reckons that I only read the bits I want to read and ignore the rest, in the same way that I only hear what I want to hear!

You may wonder how long it has taken to write this book and just how I accomplished the task. It has taken me just under a year, although seven months of that were dormant. In all probability the actual time spent writing was less than a month, but ironing things out and getting things in the right order took a lot longer. Typing it out and printing it was easy, once I got my new computer. The biggest problem is that it also has solitaire on it, and I am forever trying to beat my previous highest score – my highest to date 710! Whenever it is a typing day I always spend the first half an hour playing solitaire, much to my wife's disgust. Luckily she is not normally up when I am doing that as I am an early riser. I am fortunate in that although a good score inspires me, a bad score does not depress me. This may well be because I do not find typing difficult. I was trained as a shorthand writer in the army and still touch-type at sixty plus words a minute, which means that a book of ninety thousand words can be typed up within a matter of days. The printing is even easier. A book of one hundred and eighty pages can be printed in the time that I wash up the dishes and put them all away. Isn't modern technology wonderful! I dare not tell my wife this as she would have me writing two books a week and tell me off if I was doing anything else. I like to think that I am creative but I am not that creative. I do have a lot to say but not that much!

French children – we did not know they existed and then all of a sudden they discovered that we had a daughter their own age. It was just like the Pied Piper of Hamlyn – they all came from out of nowhere, not by their hundreds but at least half a dozen of them. They were intrigued to have a foreigner in their midst and quite surprised to find that she spoke in their native tongue! There was lots of laughter, lots of fun and many *faux pas*. There is nothing like learning French at the sharp end, in particular from children: they politely listen to everything that you have to say, nobody is embarrassed if you make a mistake and they are quite happy to tell you, slowly, how you should say something. As my daughter said, it's much more interesting than listening to tapes at school and you learn a lot faster – you have to in order to survive! They are intrigued by Le Manoir because it is so big, and they are convinced that we must be very, very rich. I haven't the heart to tell them that we are here because we are crazy, not because we are rich. They just would not understand! I am sure that my daughter is going to enjoy her holidays much more with these new-found friends. She will also enjoy introducing her English friends to them when they come over, no doubt impressing them with how good her French has become!

Birthdays. I don't know why, but mine is the only one that seems to get celebrated properly. I suppose it is because it always occurs in the Easter holidays. My wife always seems to produce complete surprises for my birthday, and there are always very pleasant ones. She seems to have a knack for it. Although mine are always pleasant (I think) they are always very predictable and somehow lack her imagination. Perhaps it's because she is always aware of what I am up to and thus I can't spring surprises on her.

My last three birthdays have been in France and they've all been very memorable. The first one was whilst we were still living in a builders' yard. Each time we came over in those early days my wife would inevitably pack something extra in the car long after I had told her that there was not room for another thing. On this particular occasion I caught her loading a picture frame into the car, carefully wrapped in a blanket.

'What on earth do you want that for,' I asked. 'We are not really ready for hanging pictures and I am quite likely to drop a beam through it.'

'It will be your problem if you do,' she said, a comment that at the time I did not think about. I said no more and we journeyed to France.

As I unloaded the car I said, 'Which picture did you bring, and where are you going to hang it?'

'Leave it wrapped up for the time being,' she said. 'It might get dusty.'

This is not the kind of comment my wife normally makes. Usually as soon as she brings something over to France she wants to look at it, and try it here and there, to see where she is going to get the best effect.

'Fine,' I said, as I had plenty of other things to do.

Two days later it was my birthday. I had almost forgotten about it, until my younger daughter reminded me that we were going to go out to dinner that evening. I knew that I would get some cards, and possibly things from Hong Kong (where my daughter was working), from Scotland, where my bekilted younger son was working and also from England, where my elder son was, but apart from that I was not expecting anything special. My daughter gave me a copy of *Parkers Wine Guide to the Wines of Bordeaux*, a super choice, and my wife gave me a gardening book. Then she said, 'Your big present is in the lounge.' Funny, I thought, I was the last one to bed last night and I didn't see any large, unfamiliar package in the lounge. What was this mysterious and well-kept secret? Despite my curiosity my wife was not going to be hurried.

'I think we will have some breakfast first,' she said, gently teasing me as she knew that I was getting impatient. I wonder why I finished my breakfast long before anyone else!

With breakfast over, my wife decided that it was time for everything to be revealed.

'Into the lounge you go,' she said.

In I went but I could see nothing new, certainly nothing resembling a birthday present. Everything was just as I had left it the night before. For once – it happens very rarely – I was lost for words, and then I could hear my wife and daughter laughing behind me.

'Do you like it?' they said with one voice.

I was sure that I would if I knew what I was looking for and, much more importantly, if I knew just where to find it. The laughter turned to hysterics.

Trying not show any impatience I said, 'Give me a clue.'

'Are you feeling cold?' my daughter said.

'No,' I said.

'Pity,' she replied.

I felt that I had solved the mystery – the blanket-covered picture frame was my birthday present, but what was it a painting of? I very carefully unwrapped it. I can honestly say that I did not have a clue as to what was going to revealed – this is the problem with a wife who uses so many different mediums! The blanket finally fell away and all was revealed. I could not believe it – it was a portrait of me! For the second time in less than ten minutes I was totally speechless. This was definitely something for the *Guinness Book of Records* as my motto is – and this will no doubt appear as my epitaph as well – 'Never knowingly lost for words!'

Quite when my wife had done the portrait I didn't know, and of course I had never done a sitting. It turned out that she had done it from a photograph of me and that she had spent several months in her studio working on it, frequently having to cover it as I put my head around the door, naturally at the wrong moment. I will possibly let you see it when it is finished. It was certainly a very well-kept secret and one well worth waiting for!

I was thrilled to bits with it and it now hangs in pride of place above the staircase. When visitors remark on it I say it was a special commission for my birthday and they comment not only on the quality of the painting but the remarkable likeness. What a talented wife I have got!

Having recovered from that, we had to work out what to do for the rest of the day and just where we were going to dine out. In a way we wanted to dine out in St-Malo, but it was rather a long way to go so inevitably we plumped for our safe favourite where we knew that we would get a warm welcome plus good food and excellent service. Should we eat out at lunchtime or in the evening? Decisions, decisions! I was hungry already, even though I had only just eaten breakfast. It looked as if it was going to have to be lunchtime.

Yes, we were bound for Le Cygne at St Hilaire – what an unimaginative lot we are! My host was there to greet us – it was almost as if he knew'

'*Votre anniversaire, Monsieur,*' he said?

Perhaps it was because I had combed my hair, was clean-shaven and was wearing a collar and tie. It's not that I am usually totally scruffy when I go there, just relaxed. We had a table in the window – a position my wife likes as not only can you see what is going on outside but you also have a good view of all the other tables. Since it was a weekday it was entirely occupied by French people quietly getting on with their business and social occasions. In the corner, with two Frenchmen, was a woman whom I had never seen before, at least I didn't think so, yet I felt that I knew her. She was not attractive but her bony features and dark hair, with too much make-up, made her stand out. It just had to be the witch with the broomstick! Sorry, you will not know who on earth I am talking about and whether or not my assumptions were correct. 'The witch with the broomstick' is the friendly, but not very complimentary, name that Pierre, of Médoc fame, gives to one of his *notaires*. Seeing her now – I was convinced that it was she – I decided he was being a bit harsh. I would have been quite happy to do business with her, obviously under the watchful eye of dear wifey who trusts me but not implicitly. I shouldn't have written that last sentence as unbeknownst to me she crept up behind me to see what I had written and this very second has swiped me with a stale baguette. That was quite painful – I wish she had used a fresh one! The trouble is she won't waste good food. Anyway, I don't with to bore you anymore. On checking later with Pierre I discovered that I had been quite correct in my guess – I really wish I was not so psychic!

I looked around again to see if there was anyone else whom I possibly recognised or who looked particularly interesting! There was just one person. He was sitting in solitary confinement, as he always did, with his bottle of Badoit water and a half bottle of claret. He was always at the same seat, at the same table – we had never eaten there when he had not been there, either at lunchtime or in the evening. Who was he, what was he? My theory was that he either owned the hotel and restaurant, and as well as being fed was keeping an eye on the standards of both the food and the waiting, or was the brother of the widow who now owned the hotel that my host ran. I hope that does not sound too complicated! I wanted a solution to this and wanted to ask my host but my wife said, 'You dare and I won't treat you to lunch with your money!' How could I possibly refuse such an offer?

Now to the serious bit. Looking at the menu, my younger daughter, now eleven, decided that she was no longer a child and should eat off the proper menu. It's going to cost me a few extra francs, but bearing in mind that it was two females against one poor defenceless male, I was not going to argue! Even though it was only the sixty-six-franc menu (nine francs to the pound then and a mere seven francs twenty centimes to the pound now!), one was able to have a three-course meal plus aperitifs. There was a choice of five different dishes for each course but I regret to say that I cannot remember what they were. All I can remember, just and with a bit of prompting, is what we had on that day and just how enjoyable it was! My wife and I started with crab tart whilst Francesca had *potage de légumes*. Absolutely delicious! We were going through a duck phase so *confit de canard* seemed more than appropriate for us whilst *petite madame* had *jambon* with bits – well, that was how she described it. Unfortunately it has now been deleted from the menu so we cannot tell you exactly what it was! I was already feeling very full but realised that there was still a pud to follow, plus of course coffee or *thé*! The accompanying wine I haven't mentioned – this is because although my host has a very comprehensive wine list I think it is quite expensive and would rather drink *vin ordinaire* there and drink the more expensive wine back at Le Manoir, purchased by the proprietor. We have a slight problem in that my wife prefers white wine whilst I prefer red. However, it's quite easy when you buy wine by the carafe – we get a quarter-carafe for madame and a third-carafe for me. Why do I have more than my wife? It's because I am older!

The meal was superb. The wine, although only *vin ordinaire*, made the whole experience very enjoyable – it made me wonder why I did not celebrate my birthday every week, or at least if not mine then somebody else's. All I can say is that it's a good job that Le Cygne is not just around the corner because if it were, we would not even need the excuse of a birthday – we would be saying either 'I am hungry' or 'I do not feel like cooking'. We might well get to that yet!

We had a walk beside the lake, close to the church, and then a leisurely drive back to Le Manoir. We had nothing else planned for the rest of the day – one does not have to work all the time and, after all it *was* my birthday!

My birthday next year, was also a surprise – not the fact that it occurred but the way that it was celebrated! I got up quite early, leaving the slumberers. When I went up to call them I was politely told to go away but to be clean-shaven and changed by 10.30 a.m. at the latest. When I asked for further information I was met with silence. Ah well, the best thing was to do as I was bid and just wait. My wife and daughter emerged on time looking very smart, fit for a garden party. Now what was going to happen?

I was told to start the car. They both climbed in and then I was told to drive West on the lower road through Lassay.

'Where are we going?' I asked.

'I don't really know,' said my wife, but I did not fully believe her. After we had passed the lovely medieval castle at Lassay, I assumed that we were going straight on and as nobody said anything that was what I did.

We reached the small town of Gorron and my wife said, 'Have you got anything for lunch?'

I was a bit surprised as that was normally her department.

'No,' I said.

'Then you had better go into Super U and get something.'

This was not turning out to be the sort of birthday that I had expected – it was not a self-catering job! What I did not know at the time was that all this had been designed to put me off the scent. Feeling a bit stunned at this stage I just picked up two pieces of cheese, a ripish Pont l'Evêque and a Petits Amis, a banana and a bottle of cider. I didn't really see what they had bought as by this time they had gone through the checkout and were back in the car. With that done, we carried on driving, to where I did not know as I was not being given any guidance. This was worse than a mystery tour! Just after twelve o'clock my wife announced that perhaps we should find a lay-by and have some lunch – how romantic!

At this stage I said, 'Just where are we going?'

The suspense continued as my wife said that she did not really know! How about visiting St-Malo? So they were planning to take me out to a meal in the old part of St-Malo – that would be nice. They were still giving nothing away, however. I enjoyed my cheese and my cider. My wife ate my solitary banana and then off we drove.

Arriving at the outskirts of St-Malo, I asked, 'Which way now?'

She told me and then, when we were within a kilometre of the old town, she suddenly said, 'Turn left.' The penny dropped. At last I knew just what the real surprise was – she had booked us into a charming little hotel where we had stayed before. It was designed more like an extended stone farmhouse, with lovely beamed ceilings but also all the mod cons! I was very impressed by their secrecy, but equally I think that they were impressed by my lack of questioning. After a bit of a relaxation, a bath and a chance for my daughter to watch a bit of Sky television – that was indeed a luxury for as yet we had no television in Le Manoir, not even a video – we took a walk in the old part of the town, watched the fire-eaters who were performing in the street and listened to an assortment of musicians. There is a very large number of restaurants in this area, all bar one serving similar sorts of food – *moules et frites*, *steak et frites* and *jambon et frites* – hardly *cordon bleu*! The one where we normally ate, and where we would no doubt be dining this evening, was the odd one out. From the outside it appeared to be the least inviting, but appearances can be deceptive. It opened at seven and it was one of those restaurants where if you were not in by seven thirty, then you stood no chance whatsoever of getting a table! We read the menu again – *moules à la crème, confit de canard,* John Dory cooked in Dijon mustard and *crème fraîche* and an assortment of very appetising sweets. I would have been quite happy to eat then but it was not yet five o'clock!

We continued our meanderings and then climbed up the steep stone stairs so that we could walk on the granite battlements which surround the old town. It's a bit breezy up there but you get a magnificent view of the harbour. There are lots of sailing boats, a merchant vessel and one of the Brittany ferries – one of those that ploughs its way from Portsmouth to St-Malo and back again and takes about eight hours to do so. It was one of their smaller ships, as the harbour is not particularly deep and, I gather, fairly difficult to navigate as well. We have never used that route but clearly if you are thinking of a short break in Normandy/Brittany it is ideal. If you just want to visit St-Malo you do not even have to bring your car as the berth is just across the road from the battlements and the old town.

We went back to the hotel to freshen up. I could not change as all I had was what I was wearing – nobody had warned me! – My wife had thoughtfully packed my pyjamas, however, and also my razor. At last it was time to eat. I could feel that my digestive juices were feeling somewhat deprived, were getting agitated and were most definitely ready for action! Having parked the car near the battlements, we went to the restaurant, which I must now describe because in some ways it is unbelievable!

On the left of a rather thin building, just the width of two rooms at the front but a bit more wedge-shaped as it goes back, is the entrance. There is a settee on the left, covered by a blanket (which looks as if it is never shaken or brushed), on which sits a poodle and sometimes one of the two older women who appear either to own it or run it. On the other side is a gateleg table and a chair, and adjoining this a parrot in a cage – or is it a parakeet? Once you have negotiated this, where the cash desk is also situated (clearly nobody is going to get out of here without paying!) you are in a restaurant that seats forty or fifty people, fairly tightly. It is very tastefully furnished with matching chairs and well-laid tables. We were the first customers that night but you must remember that I was very hungry and liable to pass out in the very near future if food did not pass my lips.

Fortunately the service was very quick. My wife and I ordered the *moules à la crème* and Francesca had the pâté. We decided on some Gros Plant from Nantes, a nice inexpensive dry white wine, to wash down our *moules* and *un Coca Cola* for you know who! Already I was feeling better. Madame had the *confit de canard* – what else, whilst I had the John Dory with a lovely Dijon mustard sauce. And *la petite madame* had *jambon* with salad and the inevitable. By the time our main dish had arrived, the restaurant was virtually full and some hopeful customers had been turned away – this was all within half an hour of their opening! The wine was going down very well and I could see that if I helped myself to another glass, my wife would be consuming her *carafe d'eau*. Even I could not possibly be that mean, so carefully reading the wine list I asked my wife what else she would like to drink. She replied, 'Just one more glass of Gros Plant,' so for me it was either water or something else. As you probably guessed I opted for the latter – a half bottle of Médoc, of vineyard unknown and non-vintage. It was a gamble but one that fortunately turned out to be very drinkable. The moral is never judge a bottle by its label! The puddings were super, as well as the coffee. We felt complete and totally relaxed. As the table was ours for the evening – nobody seems to come after that initial rush – we sat and relaxed and talked about how different things were in France when compared with England. We realised for the first time that we did not really want to live in England ever again, at least not on a permanent basis. It was a much, much easier decision to make than we had ever envisaged! Now it was time for *l'addition* – it was on our table within seconds. We filed out of the restaurant and past the grimacing madame who looked at me over her glasses in anticipation of payment. She looked pleased when I produced a bundle of notes from my wallet. They do not really like credit cards, although they accept them. Cash gives them all sorts of freedom, as they dislike TVA in the same way that the British do not like VAT. She examined the tip that I had left – a straight ten per cent – but made no comment. Her face was expressionless. Was she suggesting that perhaps this was not enough and that next time I dined there that I might leave fifteen per cent?

Who knows? We bid our *adieus* and decided that as it was quite early we would walk along the harbour front – it almost made me feel as if we were on holiday! There were lights lit on the boats as twilight approached – I suppose that small though these boats are, people stay on them within the harbour. The Brittany ferry was still there and the lack of any activity in that direction made me assume that it was not sailing until the following morning. Not a very economic way of running a ferry company, I thought. P&O keep their ferries constantly on the move, but no doubt there are good reasons, either tidal or commercial.

Our exercise completed, and now that we were not feeling quite so full, it was time to return to the hotel. We hoped to watch something good on television – I live in hope and am constantly disappointed!

Chapter XIII

The shape of our front door was absolutely magnificent, that is the space for it. Alas, all we had at the present time was a stable door patched with galvanised iron. Without putting too fine a point on it, it looked revolting! Initially I did not know what to do apart from constructing a new door (well within my capabilities according to my wife, but I was not so certain!), but time is a great provider of solutions! I removed the stable door, or rather what remained of it. The only problem that I had now was a seven-foot-high by five-foot-wide gap with nothing to fill it – and it was teatime! Fortunately fate came to the rescue. I was going through the cave when I noticed the old door, the one that separated it from the salon. It was never closed, so one tended to forget that it was there. It was the same width but unfortunately the best part of eighteen inches shorter. Still, needs must. I would have to use it for the time being. Being solid oak it was an absolute pig to move, not only getting it off its hinges but also transporting it up the cellar slope and across the salon. If I had had something else that I could have used I would willingly have abandoned it! Eventually, after about an hour of struggling, I got it to the doorway and found, as I had thought, that although the width was correct it was about fifteen inches too short. There were some rough oak planks in the barn and I nailed these on as a temporary measure, not realising at the time that they would still be there a year later and that we would still be unable to open the front door. The only entrance to the front of the house was via the cave! Having got it in an upright position, how was I going to ensure that (a) it didn't fall in and (b) it was reasonably secure when we were not around? My daughter was insisting that we attempt to make things just a little more secure.

It was at this moment that I noticed that in addition to the holes where the iron grids (windows) had been, halfway up the stone arch, on either side, were rectangular slots about four inches by three inches in size. Poking inside the one on the right I found it was partly blocked by dirt and rubble. After pulling this out with the end of a crowbar, within minutes I was able to get my arm in up to the elbow. Eventually I had a hole some four feet in depth. The other side proved to be a similar story, but it was only about eighteen inches in depth. This was clearly the way that they had barricaded themselves in, perhaps at the time of the Hundred Years' War. I was going to have no problems making my old door secure, and also the new one, when I eventually put it in.

At this stage I decided that perhaps I would attempt to hang this door temporarily to see if we could have a door that opened – that was a big mistake. As I stood on the inside and prised the bottom of the door upwards with a bit of three by two, it suddenly swung and fell. There I was, none the worse for wear but well and truly trapped, with just my head showing beyond the door. I couldn't move. Nobody seemed to be within earshot to hear my plaintive cries for help so I just lay there and waited.

Later, I do not know how much later, I heard my wife calling, 'You are very quiet, where are you?'

'Lying down,' I said.

Then she saw me, or rather just my head, and rushed over to try and help me, calling my daughter at the same time. Between the two of them they managed to raise the door and I was able to crawl from underneath it. Just imagine if I had been there on my own!

'That's that,' said my wife. 'We will place it in position, slide a beam in the two holes and leave it alone. I would rather a fixed door and you in one piece!'

She *does* value me after all!

The reason she was so concerned was that the week before, whilst I was realigning the stairs, two of the treads came away at the same time as the rail swung – when I say rail, I mean about a ton of it. I ended up on the floor underneath in a crumpled heap. Once again I was okay, although I was beginning to wonder just how many of my nine lives I had left. My wife reckoned minus three, so this is probably the reason why she decided that she was not going to let me get up to any more tricks unless she was supervising me! From now on there would be discussions and a consensus taken concerning any job of a structural nature where I might possibly come to harm.

Since then there has been only one major incident – my lives must be running out as on this occasion I broke a finger. The very old stairs to the loft slipped and came away as I was checking the water tank and I made a very rapid descent. Fortunately, as an ex-rock-climber I know how to roll, and apart from the broken finger and feeling a bit winded, I was okay. I hope and assume there will be no more instances such as those I have described as there are no more structural alterations to be undertaken, just minor modifications and artistic changes!

If anybody ever asks me again to look for a house for them in France I will most definitely say no, and here are the reasons why. Knowing how happy and contented we were with our lives in France, some friends, who were quite envious and, we thought, serious and determined people, asked us to look for something for them. Because they gave us quite clear-cut and definite specifications we took them seriously and began to comb the area and the windows of the *agences immobilières*. We even approached a friendly *notaire*.

After much time and effort we had a list of five possible properties and embarked on our visits, taking a video camera with us. We gave them a much better service than we had ever had! All the properties that we visited were interesting, but we ruled two out early on, largely because the internal decorations were terrible and they both needed a lot of time and money spent on them, even though the basic prices were quite reasonable. The other three we liked. There was a rundown watermill with its own grounds and a mill-race, together with a seven-bedroom house already converted. This was one hundred and forty thousand francs and, we felt, quite superb. The next one was a rundown chateau on five floors. It was a very thin building but it was capped by two magnificent towers. There was something rather eerie about it, but it certainly had potential. The third one was more modern and did not have much of a garden but it was tastefully done – it was the sort of property that one could move into tomorrow. Our homework done, we felt very pleased with ourselves and waited to see what our friends thought.

We had posted the video to them on the Monday and so expected to hear from them by the following weekend, but the days went by and even the weeks. After a month I decided to phone them just to check that the video had arrived!

Yes, it had arrived. It had only taken two days to reach them. Why hadn't they phoned? I wondered. I quickly got an answer, and it was certainly not the one I had expected. They said that they were sure that the properties were interesting, but that they really hadn't had time to play the video and there wasn't much point now as they didn't think they would bother to get a house in France. They had decided that England was not so bad after all!

Yet again I was speechless. I am sure that they must have heard me spluttering and guessed that I was foaming at the mouth. I seem to have had more problems with total lack of speech in France within a couple of years than I ever had in England! Then came the real sting in the tail. My friend said that he was sure that we had enjoyed doing it and that I must remind him to buy us a drink when he next saw us! I dropped the phone quickly and was still fuming half an hour later. Not only had I paid for the tape, the postage and packing and finally this telephone call, but this so-called friend had most definitely become an enemy. I could visualise sticking pins into a photograph of him, or into him himself if he were close enough. My wife thought a bullet from a Colt 45 would be much more appropriate! She is very soft and kind most of the time, but if she is taken advantage of, forget it! I wonder if this is anything to do with the fact that she is a Taurean bull?

So if somebody asks me now or in the future, I shall say that there are lots of property out here and that you should come and have a look for yourself. And in most cases I will add that you should find your own accommodation whilst you are looking! There would appear to be three types of people who say they are interested: the daydreamers, who form seventy-five per cent, and who will never venture over here to see anything, those who use it as an excuse for a free holiday without having any intentions of making a purchase (a good twenty per cent) and finally the ones who are really serious – less than five per cent. So as I only stand a one-in-twenty chance of getting it right, I am going to take the soft option and help nobody! That one in twenty probably does not need my help anyway. They know what they want, or at least have a fair idea, and they get on with it. These are the ones who I can relate to – people who get up off their backsides and get on with it, causing things to happen!

Piles of money! Wouldn't it be nice to have piles of money, preferably a big pile, or even to be able to make your own money? Well today, as a result of a conversation with one of the locals, I think I may have cracked it. In the dim and distant past, I haven't quite cracked it yet, the first money produced in Javron was made by le Duc de Bresnières within our buildings, so perhaps I have got banking in the family after all! Quite what it was like, when it was produced and how much I have yet to work out but I now feel that a metal detector might be a good investment. I don't suppose for one minute that we are sitting on a gold mine, but you never know your luck!

This house is full of constant surprises. Still I suppose when you remember it has been here for nearly one thousand years then it is not surprising! So was this before the monks, or after the monks or when the monks were here? Is this the reason why the front entrance had to be so well protected? I reckon we may well find a portcullis yet, or even a drawbridge. Now the search for the tunnel becomes even more important because if there *is* any buried treasure, or the remains of any coinage then surely that is where it is going to be! But still, even if there isn't any I suppose I could claim the title of Duc de Bresnières. I wonder if they have lords of the manor as they do in England? I rather fancy that, particularly as my chances of a knighthood are even less than zilch!

The Mayenne is full of history. There are some wonderful Roman remains, which in turn have been built on a Celtic site and castles not by the score but by the hundred. In the Mayenne area there are more than five hundred inhabited castles and goodness knows how many derelict ones.

The longer you live here, the more you realise just how many old buildings there are in the area and just how much it is steeped in history. There are times when you begin to feel that Le Manoir is almost a new building, although in its defence I must say that I doubt that there are many buildings in the area, possibly even within the Mayenne, that have had such a rich and varied history. But there is a lot more research to be done on that yet. Lots of the locals have all sorts of little bits of information about it. It isn't getting them all together that is the problem but the recording of all the snippets and trying to remove the folk lore and record just the facts, not that the former would not be interesting.

To date, we have not visited a single castle in Mayenne, although we have on more than one occasion walked around the outside of the magnificent chateau at Lassay and the adjoining rose garden, which is very beautiful when in full flower.

It was for this very reason, one Sunday in August, some two years after our purchase, that we decided to visit the Roman remains at Jubulaine – a small town just to the east of Mayenne itself. Why choose a Sunday, you may ask. Well, just as in England, there is a charge for visiting all monuments, ruins, art galleries etc: that are owned or controlled by the state, but not on Sundays! However, what we did not know was that on this particular Sunday there was a flower festival, complete with processions and marching bands and hordes and hordes of people lining the streets, all in a very jovial mood. The streets were all decorated and the locals were hanging out of their windows, taking part in a way that only the French can! The bars were full to overflowing, both the temporary ones and the permanent ones, and there was that lovely smell of sausages cooked over an open barbecue. Cooked over charcoal they always smell, and taste, that much better.

Alas, there are no amusing or funny incidents to report as when I am out with the family I am like a dog on a lead – I am kept well under control, having to behave myself and not get up to any mischief or talk too much to the locals. Never mind, it's good to be controlled sometimes!

Although the main part of the remains is only a matter of yards from the centre of the town, there was virtually nobody there. There were very clear drawings and diagrams of just how the buildings had looked. None of them were roofed – very different to the Roman baths in Bath but interesting nonetheless! Unfortunately there was no conducted tour on the day we were there. If there had been I think we would have got a lot more out of it. It's most definitely worth a second visit, perhaps when we do not have the distraction of the flower festival.

Now there is one story or visit that I *must* tell you about. It is not directly related to the Mayenne but to Le Mont St Michel, which as you already know is very relevant to my book, and in particular to the history of Le Manoir.

As you are probably aware, Le Mont St Michel is the second most visited place in France, the *most* visited being the Eiffel Tower. So as you can well imagine, almost any time you go there it is very crowded, unless you go there on a very wet and windy February day, and even then there will be plenty of cars in the car park. Ideally it is best to go there in May or October just as darkness falls. Then the whole of it is lit up and you can weave your children fantastic tales, as I remember we did with ours. They believed them until they were eleven or twelve!

Anyway, although we were well aware of this, we went in the middle of August for this visit. We wanted to look at the fireplace in the restaurant at the entrance by the drawbridge, as our main fireplace is a replica of it. We also wondered if we would see any monks with dirty feet. Our prayers were answered twofold – we saw the fireplace *and* the monks, but I will come to that in a minute.

Normally when you visit Le Mont St Michel you go over the drawbridge, under the portcullis and through two enormous doors. It's important that you go in this way as immediately beyond the doors are the loos. But on the day we visited it was not to be our lucky day – there was a diversion! We had to go via a long winding route, through the *gendarmerie*, up past the battlements and to the abbey itself, which we did not really want to visit as we had visited it before. Crisis! No loos! Then I spied a pay-as-you-go. It cost one franc, but my wife would have paid ten francs. There was a formidable queue but beggars can't be choosers. Five minutes later my wife reappeared, relieved but in hysterics. Whilst she had been queuing two men had come in to use the facilities (separate, I hasten to add!). The madame who was running it had been in there, sitting on a camp chair drinking her coffee and no doubt checking her takings, which on a hot day like this must have been quite considerable! She had told the two men that they could use the facilities but that they would have to wait until she had finished her coffee. Just imagine drinking coffee in those surroundings! My wife had paid her money and beat a hasty retreat. Surely this could only happen in France!

The whole isle was absolutely heaving. There were people of all shapes and sizes and of all nationalities, licking ice creams, drinking cans of Coke and other fizzy drinks, a flock of camcorders and even more cameras. People were taking pictures of people taking pictures of people – I would love to see some of the results. The gift shops and the restaurants on the winding hill were just the same as on our first visit more than twenty-five years ago, but no doubt the prices had increased considerably. We visited the church halfway down the hill as we had fond memories of it – our elder three children lit a candle in there fourteen years ago to bring good luck to the unborn baby, whom, fourteen years later, they all idolise. I wish I had been in that fortunate position when I was growing up!

My wife, daughter and her friend succumbed to whippy ice creams whilst I was totally abstinent! I am not a great lover of ice cream really. Then we continued our way down the hill, pushing and jostling with twice as many coming up as were going down. I had thought that this was a one-way system, but then realised it was after six o'clock – the guards had gone home and now it was a free-for-all. We just wanted to examine as closely as possible this fireplace. We were there – La Mare Poulan. We have not eaten there before, although most other famous people have. Was that a slip of the tongue or do I have delusions (someone once rudely said 'illusions'!) of grandeur? Anyway, as we went inside, the head waiter came over immediately, thinking that we had come to dine. The fireplace is just inside the door and there was the chef (or whatever his title is!) cooking an omelette in an enormous copper frying pan over the glowing embers.

'That's your job tonight,' I said to my wife.

What she said is totally unrepeatable, but I did realise that if I wanted an omelette that night then *I* would have to cook it. Fortunately, soufflé omelettes are my speciality so that was not going to be a problem. I was feeling mean and would cook one just for me, however! One has to assert one's authority occasionally!

Much to our surprise, although the fireplace here was absolutely identical to ours, ours was one and half or even twice the size! No, that does *not* mean that I have to produce even bigger soufflé omelettes for non-paying guests. Now if I'm charging, then that's different! I then realised that I had run out of film so there was no opportunity to record this moment. Ah well, we had an excuse for another visit. Perhaps we would even eat in the restaurant, but most definitely out of season. Turning around, I suddenly saw three monks walking towards us – thank you, up above – and they were shoeless. Not only that but I could see that their feet were dirty. I was tempted to ask them if they would like to wash them on my slab, obviously providing them with a jug of water, but discretion is the better part of valour.

One thing that did intrigue me was that their habits were grey and not brown – I had always assumed that they were Franciscan Friars. Clearly they weren't, unless the dye had run. But if not, then what were they? Obviously a bit more research needs to be done!

I felt totally and utterly exhausted but the worst was still to come. We had to get out of the car park! Getting in is easy as they funnel you in at the far end through four paying gates and marshal you to one of five areas, getting you away from the paying booths as quickly as possible so as not to interrupt or interfere with the cash flow – which on a day like that must have been colossal. No wonder they can afford free entry into the isle itself! Obviously there is no charge for the exit so they do not control it and leave it as a free-for-all. There are signs saying 'Sortie' but just which lane you choose and how you negotiate things are entirely up to you. There are five lanes which merge into three, and then into two and finally into one, with nobody controlling anything. The French drivers give way to nobody, not even their own kind. The English (well, most of them!) are polite and get taken advantage of. They wave one car through and before they know where they are, six more have followed. The Belgians drive at you and make the assumption that you will keep out of their way, which if you have any sense you will do – most people do. The Germans drive forcefully, but sensibly whilst the Italians and the Spaniards are totally unpredictable!

If you had seen me driving on the day, judging from the above description (ignoring my GB plates) you would have found it difficult to decide just what nationality I was as I used the best and worst of all of them!

That journey of a mile – half a mile towards Le Mont St Michel and half a mile back, so that we were parallel to where we had started – took us three-quarters of an hour. The problem is that since you are on a peninsular you have absolutely no alternatives. As I said earlier, unless I come back totally out of season I am not coming back, and if, sorry, *when*, friends come to stay I shall provide them with a map and even volunteer to pay the parking charge just to avoid going there!

So it had been an interesting day, definitely an exhausting day. We did not have any new information, however. I need to do some more research if I am going to prove the tie between Le Mont St Michel and Le Manoir. I *know* that it exists – I can just feel it – but for the purists and disbelievers, of which I am sure there are many – knowing is just not enough!

It was nice to get back to the peace and tranquillity of Le Manoir and to complete the day I played a CD of Gregorian chants!

Sad things happen over the course of time, and I suppose that one of the saddest events that has happened since we first came to the Mayenne was the death of the proprietor of our local restaurant. What can one say apart from the fact that we felt privileged to eat in his restaurant and we feel sure that due to the expertise he passed on to his son it will continue to flourish over the years and well into the Millennium! Death is the one thing that we are never prepared for, the thing that we know is inevitable but always imagine happening only to other people.

But as both grannies, and most certainly my most beloved godmother would have said, 'Eat, drink and be merry, for tomorrow we die.' All of them were fatalists and, fortunately, I am too. You can say what you would *like* to happen tomorrow, but even with the best planning in the world you cannot be sure that it will – life is so unpredictable! I remember talking to an octogenarian once who said that every further day that he survived was worth at least another two, and so on, on an accumulative scale! He actually lived to be a hundred and four and was one of the few, if not the only person, alive when I was young who had seen Isambard Kingdom

Brunel standing on the Clifton Suspension Bridge the day it was completed. He could even remember crossing the Avon Gorge in a basket, pulled across on an iron cable, prior to that!

Opposite the house, partly behind the barn, is a huge cider press. It rests on its side, and in that position it is difficult to work out just how it operates, although no doubt it is very simple. One day, assuming that I can find enough apples, I am going to use it. No, I am not going to ask Madame Foghorn – I would rather do without the cider! It is quite massive. The base is solid oak and is about four feet square. In the middle of this is a giant threaded screw, a couple of inches wide and six feet in height, and then there is the wheel to wind the press down and so compress the apples. I've just realised that I now know how to operate it! There will be no holding me back now – it will be my new toy for the autumn.

The cloths, or rather the sacking (specially made and much stronger than ordinary sacking!) were all in the attic when we arrived. There were all hanging over ropes waiting to be used. The wooden pieces which make the frame rigid, and which interlock with each other and number some three dozen, were stacked in the cave. But alas there were no cider barrels, just a huge quantity of hoops. Perhaps they made their own barrels, a job which I feel would require far too much skill for me!

Quite how I am going to move it I really don't know. In most cases, when moving things that are heavy and bulky, I just resort to simple physics – levers and mechanical advantages, etc. But this is of mammoth proportions! Standing back and looking at it recently I did not reckon that even two harnessed shire-horses could move it, but that was a non-starter anyway as there are none of those around! I could, I suppose, contact the vet! On second thoughts, no! What we will have to do is gather all the cider apples in and have the cloths and frame all ready for assembly. We'll have Acker Bilk playing 'Drink up Ye Cider George', as he did at the Crown and Dove in Bristol in the fifties, and a load of my friends over to heave the whole thing into position. I reckon the cost of the cider would be about fivepence a pint but it would be worth it!

My knowledge of cider-making is limited to being a hands-on helper more than twenty years ago when we lived in Somerset. Close to the old farmhouse where we lived was a farmhouse inhabited by Cyril and Daisy – no, they were not husband and wife but cousins. We used to see more of Cyril than Daisy, as Daisy had trouble with her feet. When she was herding in the cows – done, I am sure, under protest – she would always be wearing carpet slippers!

The farm was not very efficient but they produced enough milk to survive. The cider was just the icing on the cake. Incidentally, it was Cyril's farm that was virtually the last one in the county, if not the country, to have a milk-churn collection. Just four churns a day!

Although we lived in a relatively isolated and small community – just four houses/farms – it must have been well over a year before I was introduced/invited into the cider club. Strangers clearly had to prove themselves! I had noticed that at weekends, particularly Sunday mornings before lunch, there would be a marked increase in traffic in the lane. There would be three cars an hour instead of one or even none! I must confess that I did not take much notice but when I received my invitation I realised why!

Up the road from us, Cyril used to tie a piece of string across the lane, with a plastic bag attached to the middle to prevent the cows from wandering down towards us and then on to the main road. It worked well with the locals, as they always retied it after passing through, but strangers didn't bother – they probably thought that it was some children playing!

One day the cows escaped and I found them nibbling my hedge. It was a good job it was not yew – I wonder just who would have been liable if it had been. Then I looked up and there was Cyril standing up on the brow of the hill, with his hands on his hips. I waved and he waved back, and then I realised that he was asking if I would be so kind as to drive the cows back. I did and met him at the top of the hill, smiling.

'Thirsty work,' he said. 'Fancy a mug of cider?'

How could I refuse such a welcome offer? It was then that I was invited into the inner sanctum! In the two barns beyond the cow stalls, where I had never been before, I became aware of the lovely aroma of cider apples and then saw the biggest barrels that I have ever seen. Were they seventy-two gallons or a hundred and forty-four gallons? I just could not estimate.

'Don't really know,' said Cyril, although I am not sure that I really believed him. Beneath his wide-eyed innocence and apparent naiveté was a very shrewd individual, who was happy to talk about the green pound and who was quite knowledgeable about European agricultural policy.

Enough of all that – it was tasting time! Cyril poured a pint into an earthenware mug for me, using a bit of hosepipe with a tap on the end, and one for himself. It was real journeyman's cider, neither sweet nor rough and slightly green in colour – best, I would imagine, with a good chunk of bread and a lump of cheddar cheese. I was in my element, particularly when offered a second mugful. I hoped that the cows would escape regularly now when I was home. I even had the idea of cutting the piece of string to ensure that they did but I reckoned that Cyril might not fall for that one or not give me my reward if I brought the cows back.

As it turned out this was not going to be necessary. Not only had I been accepted into the club, which meant that I could buy cider at fifty pence a gallon, but I was also going to assist him in making it! Thus started, and continued, a very happy friendship, in which I helped him with the cider press. In some ways it was more modern than the one that I have now as it was driven by an old Model-T Ford engine, with belts that constantly slipped and also broke from time to time. You would be quietly working when Cyril would suddenly say, 'Duck!' and one of the belts would go flying past an ear. I can't say that the Health and Safety would have been very happy with that!

One day when I was there he had a visit from Customs and Excise over a small point of duty. This little man, who it later turned out was a customer (had he been secretly watching and making notes each time he came to purchase his cider?), called one Saturday afternoon when I was there to say that Cyril was liable to pay excise duty and that he had brought the necessary forms for him to fill in! Cyril was totally unmoved as he knew exactly just how much he could produce without having to pay duty. Pushing his cap to the back of his head and chewing on a bit of straw, he said that he produced one thousand four hundred and ninety-nine gallons, and three quarts.

'And this is yer mugful,' he added, holding it temptingly

beneath the man's waiting mouth and then quickly taking it away. Almost with fire in his eyes, he said, 'If you try and make me pay duty then you get no more bloody cider.' With his tail between his legs, the man disappeared somewhat sheepishly, and it must have been a month or more before he returned to buy cider. But from then on no mention of duty was ever brought into the conversation. Those were the days in England! Fortunately it is still like this in France today.

Talking of rules and regulations reminds me of a very recent visit to Le Cygne. We went late one lunchtime and I was greeted by the lovely smell of cigars wafting through the door. Although my wife is anti-smoking she can still appreciate the aroma of a nice cigar. She even knows the difference between a Wintermanns and a fine Havana. The latter, of course, so they say, and who am I to disbelieve it, is rolled out on a female Cuban thigh – where do I get my stories from! Anyway, much as I was enjoying the aroma, I was surprised as more than a year ago the French put a ban on smoking in all public places, including restaurants. I drew my host to one side and asked him why.

He shrugged his shoulders and said, 'It is a bad law and we only obey good laws.' They react in the same way if there is a new agriculture policy they do not like – they block the roads and empty their vegetables until they get some action. With the smoking there is no need to do anything because nobody seems to be trying to enforce anything.

Leading on from this, I remembered that in recent times the alcohol limit for driving has been lowered. I asked my host, as he showed us to our table how this had affected his sales. 'It is good,' he said. 'We sell less cheap wine and more expensive wine.' There is a moral in that somewhere! I suppose he meant that he sold more expensive wine than he used to, where the profit margins are much greater, but a smaller volume overall. That is my simple solution, but knowing how illogical the French can be, I could be totally wrong! I think that is yet another thing I like about France. Whereas in England you feel that you are totally controlled or are being dictated to, in France you almost feel that these are only recommendations, and that as long as you only extend the law or break it to a minor degree there will not be any problems. As a result I am sure that everyone is a lot happier! If only the government, and big organisations would understand that the more restrictions you impose, the more problems you get. People will forever be looking for ways of beating the system. It reminds me of a company for which I used to act as an advisor. When they were asked by prospective employees if they had any rules and regulations by which they had to abide, the MD used to say that they had just one: 'We all work together to maximise profit and our target is ten per cent per annum increase.' This is nice and simple and something that they have easily achieved for fifteen years. In that time they have actually achieved nearly double that!

Now I must talk about the treadmill. It is situated just behind the cider press, albeit in a permanent position. It consists of a circular granite ring, which is two feet in height and about eight feet in diameter, with a larger (in diameter, that is) granite ring outside it – probably twelve feet in diameter. Around, or rather within, the two granite rings runs a granite grinding wheel which is fixed on the end of a wooden beam and which was, presumably, driven by horsepower. We think it was designed for grinding corn and that with local taxes the farmer (in the past) was allowed to keep a certain amount of grain for making into bread, hence our large bread oven. It is certainly far too big just for the farm – it must have been for the whole neighbourhood as well! The bread oven is seven feet in diameter and I reckon that even in one baking session you could produce a minimum of sixty baguettes or a lesser number of *pains*! I have asked everyone in the neighbourhood and not one person can remember, or has been told, anything about a large bread-making concern going on in the area. It is a total mystery! Perhaps it was only something that went on in the Middle Ages.

Being the romantic that I am, I would dearly like to get the bread oven working again and fancy going into competition with the local *boulangerie*, or getting my wife to make her lovely malt loaves. I dare not mention this at the moment, however, as it is most certainly not on her priority list. Most definitely the house and living accommodation come first. The bread oven is not even relegated to second place, but is last by a very long way. Ah well, perhaps I shall manage it one day!

Our work goes on – one wonders just how much progress one

had made and will we ever finish our project. Our friends, particularly our French ones, encourage us and say such nice things as, 'You have achieved so much in such a short time.' The photographs that we have taken confirm that we have achieved a lot but alas none of these help us with our timescale. The initial timescale of five years has come and alas gone.

I comfort myself by saying, 'Does it matter?' We are enjoying ourselves – well, most of the time.

My wife tries to reassure me by saying, 'Our problems will begin when we have finished – what will we do then?'

'Move slowly across the room on my zimmer,' I reply.

As a result of this I make no further forecast as to when it will be finished but I am sure that we will continue to enjoy living in the Mayenne and no doubt have many other amusing experiences.